Secrets of the Heart

Patti Shenberger

CRIMSON
ROMANCE
F+W Media, Inc.

Published by
Crimson Romance
an imprint of F+W Media, Inc.
10151 Carver Road, Suite 200
Blue Ash, Ohio 45242

www.crimsonromance.com

Dedication

This book is dedicated to all the doctors and nurses who helped me through a very difficult time in my life when I wasn't sure if I was going to make it or not. To all of you, thank you for keeping my spirits lifted and my body in one piece.

Any errors in this book are all mine.

Prologue

Isabelle fairly flew across the busy intersection in her haste to make the traffic signal, the folded white piece of paper clenched tightly in her fist. She couldn't wait to get home and tell Nicholas the news as soon as he arrived back from his interview at the hospital. Granted it wasn't anything they had planned. They'd certainly spoken about it over the course of the past year, but both had agreed to wait until their careers were on track. But this...this was definitely an unexpected surprise. And one she couldn't wait to share with Nicholas. Giving a cursory glance to the black stretch limousine parked at the curb in front of the apartment building, she noticed the driver lounged against the side of the vehicle, his dark suit and mirrored sunglasses a contrast to the blue-jean-clad students walking down the street carrying oversized backpacks.

In fact, both he and the car looked decidedly out of place in the quiet neighborhood. The converted brownstone and adjacent older buildings normally drew a more studious type of resident, as pretty much all the tenants were either finishing up their last year of college, or in their first year of residency at the nearby hospital facility. She and Nicholas were lucky to get in when they did. Nicholas found a medical student who needed to sublet the one bedroom apartment, making it possible for them to avoid staying in their tiny, cramped basement studio for another year. This one gave them all the extra space they needed, for the time being that was.

Isabelle took the flight of stairs as quickly and carefully as she could, coming to a stop outside their apartment. The door was partially ajar and Isabelle could hear the sound of footsteps walking back and forth across the polished hardwood floors. She slowly pushed open the door and peered around the frame. Normally her day ended earlier than his most afternoons.

Nicholas walked out of the bedroom carrying an armload of clothes. Obviously back from the interview before she'd managed to get home, he headed toward the couch and placed them in an empty suitcase. His tie was askew and his shirtsleeves rolled up to the elbows. Then he turned back toward the bedroom as though to repeat the process. Next to the suitcase was a duffel bag, presently half full of textbooks.

Isabelle walked into their apartment and looked around. A myriad of suitcases and boxes littered the floor, each containing a portion of Nicholas's belongings.

"Nicholas?" She came to a halt next to the sofa and stared down into the suitcase. "What are you doing?"

"I have to leave." He strode briskly into the room and deposited another load of clothes and some toiletries into the piece of luggage before retreating back to the bedroom. She heard the sound of the dresser drawers opening and shutting.

"I don't understand." Isabelle quickly shoved the piece of paper in her pocket and lowered herself to the arm of the sofa. "Has something happened?"

"My mother is ill. I must return home at once." His brusque tone offered no comfort.

He never stopped packing, and Isabelle began to get a sinking feeling in the pit of her stomach. She gnawed on her lower lip and watched as he filled one box full of books, then zipped the suitcase shut and handed both off to the man who now stood waiting at the door of the apartment. The same man Isabelle had seen minutes before downstairs at the curb.

"Thank you, Gus." Nicholas turned back toward her. "I have made arrangements for the rent to be paid through the rest of the school year, as well as the utilities. Within a few weeks, I'll send for the rest of my things. I don't have time to pack it all today. I apologize for the short notice, Isabelle."

"What about us?" She unconsciously smoothed her hand across the front of her coat, both knowing and fearing the answer before he even said a word. A feeling of unease rippled through her as Isabelle fought down the urge to run to him, throw her arms around him and never let go.

Nicholas shook his head and her stomach plummeted even further. "I must go. My family needs me." He grabbed his jacket from the chair and shoved his arms through the sleeves, then swung the backpack up on his shoulder.

For a brief second he paused as if to say something, then Nicholas softly kissed her cheek, and was out the door, shutting it firmly behind him.

Isabelle heard his footsteps retreat down the stairs and then the sound of the main door closing behind him. She walked to the living room window and stared out. Below, she could see Nicholas saying something to the driver. She rested her hand against the glass and willed him to look up at her. To lift his hand, to smile at her, to do anything…

"Please look up at me. Just let me know everything will be all right. Please Nicholas…"

He climbed into the back seat of the limousine as the driver closed the door behind him. Seconds later, the sleek black vehicle pulled away from the curb and was soon out of sight down the street.

"But I need you too," Isabelle whispered, the heavy weight of dread wrapping itself tightly around her in a vise grip. She leaned forward, rested her forehead on the cool picture window, and continued her vigil.

Isabelle wasn't positive how long she stood there waiting for the car to come back, hoping and praying it would and at the same time knowing it wasn't meant to be. Finally, she took off her coat and draped it on the back of the chair, then moved to the corner of the sofa. Sitting down, she kicked off her shoes and curled her legs up underneath her. With a heavy sigh, she wrapped the worn, brown crocheted afghan around her shoulders and closed her eyes, willing the tears not to fall.

When she next opened them, the room was dark and the streetlights were on outside the windows. Shadows from passing headlights danced across the walls, bathing the room in a sporadic pattern. She didn't know how long she'd been sitting there or even what time it was. Truthfully, Isabelle didn't care. With Nicholas gone, none of it mattered any more.

Stretching out her stiff legs, she moved her feet to the floor. That's when she felt the first twinge. A slight cramp danced its way across the front of her abdomen, squeezing her from side to side. Followed by a second, then a rapid succession of many more, each more painful than the previous one. Sweat beaded her forehead as she gripped the arm of the sofa for support and tried to stand. Isabelle bit her lip in order to work through the pain. The newest wave felt as though someone had plunged a knife into her stomach and wrenched it downward. She splayed her hands across her navel and clenched her teeth, forcing down the nausea that threatened.

Isabelle managed to get to her feet and gasped. The pain now so strong it doubled her over immediately. Taking a few shaky steps forward, she became aware of the warm wetness between her thighs. Her mind raced through the possibilities as she reached over and turned on the lamp on the end table, knocking her purse to the floor in the process.

There was blood, so much bright red blood, soaked clear through her jeans. Panic clouded her thoughts as she fumbled in her purse for her cell phone. Fighting the rising fear, she tried to steady her trembling fingers as she punched in three numbers and waited for an operator to pick up.

"Please help me. I think I'm having a miscarriage." She rattled off the apartment address, and then tried to quell her racing nerves as she waited for help to arrive. Sinking to the floor, she closed her eyes and prayed for a miracle. But deep in her heart, Isabelle knew it was already too late to save her unborn baby.

Chapter One

Spring 2012

Isabelle pulled open the door of the cardiac care department offices and walked quickly across the threshold. It was hard to believe over nine years had passed since she hired in at Garner General Hospital. In that time, so many changes had occurred that Isabelle felt the need to remind herself on a daily basis how lucky she was to have secured the position of caridothroacic surgeon within these four walls. Today, though, there seemed to be more staff than necessary milling about the department.

"Good morning, Doctor Tandori."

"Good morning, Eleanor." She took the stack of message slips from her secretary and looked around the hall. "Anything I need to be aware of this morning?"

"Doctor Aldridge came through about twenty minutes ago looking for you. Apparently, there's a big shot in town touring the hospital and Doctor A wanted you to accompany them. He seemed very much on edge this morning when he was here as though he expected you to already be in the office. I reminded him you were doing rounds and he asked that you call him as soon as you returned to the office."

"I can well imagine. As much as he loves touting the hospital, I think it also drives him crazy being pulled away from the action. Thanks, I'll touch base with him in a few minutes."

Doctor Kevin Aldridge, chief of staff of Garner General Hospital and a man one hundred percent committed to his craft. If anyone deserved to be heralded for his dedication, Kevin would be at the top of the list. He had been Isabelle's mentor and to date she was still struck by the compassion and caring he showed for his previous patients. Something she hoped she exuded in her own work.

"Rumor has it whoever the visitor is, he's quite a hunk," Eleanor added with a wink.

Isabelle stared at her fifty-plus-year-old secretary. The woman never gossiped, never shared details of her personal life, and never said a bad word about anyone. Her usually reserved demeanor was a direct contrast to the words just spoken and the twinkle that lit her gaze as she smiled at Isabelle.

"That's an interesting observation, Eleanor. I'll make note of it," Isabelle replied, shaking her head fondly at the woman.

"You should, it's high time you found yourself a man. Take a night off, go to dinner, then take the weekend off and go somewhere wonderful. Sit in the sun, have a drink or two or more, and forget about this place for a few hours. You deserve more than this." Eleanor waved her hand around in a large arc.

"Thanks but..." The rest of the words caught in her throat.

Eleanor sighed. "I know your work is your life. Mark my words: one day you're going to wake up and find you want better than this. I'm just saying." The phone rang and Eleanor quickly picked up the call.

Isabelle let herself into her office and closed the door behind her, depositing her briefcase on the credenza. Settling herself in her desk chair, she leaned back and thought about what Eleanor had said. Would she one day regret the choices she'd made for her life? Isabelle shook her head in denial. Of course she wouldn't. She loved her work, was dedicated to her patients, and spent every day and every weekend working to make sure they got back on their feet and resumed their lives.

If that meant she was a workaholic, so be it. There were far worse things to be called in life. And if it helped her to forget the past, then all the better.

Looking down, she glanced at each message in turn. Two from patients, two from the hospital laboratory, and one very descriptive message from her mother reminding her of her parents

11

upcoming plans to fly to Guatemala the following morning to work with the local mission to build a school. Isabelle crumpled the pink paper into a tight ball and threw it in the trash. Keeping her parents at arm's length was the best way to avoid the pain that came with their cold and unfeeling attitude toward their only child. It was as though her being born had ruined everything that was good in their lives. Yet with everyone else, they were sweet and generous. The farther away her parents were the better was the mantra Isabelle now lived by. And it had served her quite nicely.

She reached for the phone and punched in Kevin's extension, then sat back to reread the other messages.

"Good morning, Mary. Is Doctor Aldridge available? Eleanor tells me he was here in the department looking for me."

"I'm sorry, Doctor Tandori, but he's still out escorting a visitor through the hospital at present. Doctor Aldridge was very much hoping to catch up with you before you went into surgery this morning. I'll have him return the call when he finishes the tour."

Isabelle blew out of a soft sigh and looked at her watch. "I'm heading into pre-op in about twenty minutes. Please let him know that whatever it is will have to wait until later, I'm afraid. Thank you, Mary."

None of the other visitors to the hospital had ever shown the slightest interest in her department or her, so why now? Whatever the reason, Isabelle pushed it firmly from her mind as she hung up the phone and swiveled to face the windows overlooking the common area. The snow continued to fall in thick, wet flakes, carpeting the ground. Maybe it was time to think about getting away for a weekend, someplace warm, someplace exciting, someplace… With a sigh, Isabelle turned from the window. Even if she had somewhere to go, whom would she go with? It wasn't like she had a bevy of close girlfriends to call up and suggest a girls' weekend away. Maybe it was time to face up to the fact that her job was her life. Better just to forget what she couldn't have and move on with what she could. Lifting the sheet of paper from her desk, Isabelle studied the day's surgical schedule.

Whatever Kevin needed would have to be put on the back burner for the time being. Her patients were her first concern this morning, as they were each and every morning. And Isabelle knew he wouldn't expect any less of her. She dropped the rest of the messages on the blotter and pushed back her chair. Time to begin her day.

*

Isabelle tied the lower half of her mask across the back of her neck, for the moment leaving the top half hanging down. She scanned the medical file the nurse handed her one last time before heading into pre-op. Her first patient of the day, Anthony Frank, age seventy-two, had been complaining of chest pain, fatigue, and shortness of breath. Prior examination showed an abnormal heartbeat on top of present symptoms. Conferring with his general physician and reviewing previous tests and lab work, Isabelle suspected he was suffering from myocarditis, an inflammation of the heart muscle. Today, he was scheduled for an endomyocardial biopsy. Her team was already in place and the procedure would begin momentarily.

She walked through the doors of the surgical suite and headed toward the head of the table, handing the chart off to the head nurse.

"Good morning, Anthony, how are you doing this morning?"

The man on the surgical table smiled up at her, his features pale under the bright lights of the sterile room. "Have to admit, doc, I've had better days."

Isabelle smiled at him and patted his arm. "And soon you will again. Do you have any questions on what we're going to do today? Anything you're concerned about before we start?"

He shook his head. "No, let's just get it over with so I can go home."

She lifted her gaze to the anesthesiologist and gave a slight nod. "We're going to give you a local anesthesia to numb the side of your neck. You're going to be awake for the procedure, and the most you'll feel is some pressure. I want you to let me know if you feel any pain, or anything else, okay."

Anthony nodded, turning his head for the nurse to clean his neck. He closed his eyes and a low sigh escaped his lips. "Ready when you are, Doctor Tandori."

Isabelle took her position and accepted the syringe from the nurse. She cleared her mind and focused on the patient before her. Nothing mattered except him.

A few seconds later, she lifted her head and looked at her patient. "How are you doing, Anthony?"

"Fine, stings a bit though."

"That's normal. It will subside in a few minutes."

Isabelle made the initial incision, inserted the sheath, and then threaded the catheter through and into the blood vessel. Once she reached the right ventricle, she turned slightly to examine the x-ray monitor. The bioptome was exactly where she wanted it. She took several pieces of the heart muscle, no larger than the size of a pinhead. and placed them in the sterile containers.

She handed off the samples to the technician and turned back to Anthony. "Almost done. Hang in there, you're doing great."

Movement off to her left caught Isabelle's attention and she lifted her gaze away from her patient. Two men stepped into the room and stood just inside the door. Both wore scrubs and surgical masks covered their faces. The first she recognized, the second had his gaze averted from hers, but something about the way the man carried himself put her senses on edge.

"Doctor Aldridge, you know I don't allow visitors during procedures." Isabelle purposely kept her voice low.

"I'm certain you can make an exception this time, Doctor Tandori." Kevin's voice brooked no argument.

Isabelle swallowed the retort and shook her head, her eyes narrowed as she glared at Kevin over the top of her surgical mask. Around her, the surgical team was casting concerned glances among her, Dr. Aldridge, and the stranger. Very rarely did Isabelle voice a complaint during a procedure or surgery, even more rare would it be in a public setting, such as now. She preferred to address an issue one-on-one, in private, away from prying eyes and listening ears. The last thing she needed was a distraction, especially during a surgical procedure. Distractions caused mistakes and mistakes could be deadly. Something she never tolerated when it came to the matter of life or death.

The second man turned, providing a clear view of his face, and Isabelle started. A pair of vivid blue eyes stared back at her above his mask and an icy shiver skittered down her spine. Her hand trembled slightly as she refocused her gaze on the patient lying before her on the table and blocked the other man out of her thoughts. Slowly withdrawing the catheter, she applied a piece of gauze, and then placed a bandage over the incision.

"Anthony, we're all finished. How are you feeling?"

"Doing good, Doc. Glad to know it's over." His voice was softer than before, causing Isabelle to take a quick look at his vitals. All were well within normal ranges considering the circumstances, though his features were still pale.

Isabelle smiled down at Anthony and squeezed his shoulder. "Good. You close your eyes and rest now. They're going to take you to post-op. I'll see you there shortly, and we'll talk later."

After Anthony was wheeled from the surgical suite, Isabelle strode quickly from the room, her anger palpable as the two men followed behind her.

She whirled around, furious with Kevin for compromising her authority in front of her team. Without giving him a chance to speak, she pulled off her gloves, then her mask, and threw them in the trash receptacle. Reaching behind her, Isabelle untied the strings of her surgical gown, yanking the sleeves down and off her arms in rapid succession.

"What were you thinking, bringing someone in there without my knowledge or permission, Kevin? I don't allow anyone in the room who doesn't expressly belong there. Anyone other than my surgical team needs to be personally vetted by me. Unless something has changed and I haven't been informed, the rules are still the same." Granted, by verbally attacking the man she was doing in private what she never would have done in public.

Kevin raised his hand to stop her protest. "Isabelle, allow me to explain. Nothing has changed and under normal conditions, I wouldn't compromise your rules. Today we have a different situation. This is Prince Nicholas Corsairs of Wellfleet Isle. He's here in the States for a very specific reason. One that involves you, or I wouldn't have allowed him access to the surgical suite."

Isabelle threw a startled glance to the man now leaning casually against the wall, stripping off his surgical gown.

Prince Nicholas Corsairs?

He smiled at her as he lowered his mask and her heart skipped a beat. Darn it all, she didn't want to have any reaction to him, but even after all these years her body still betrayed her. She knew exactly who he was from the moment their eyes met and it hadn't lessened the impact of seeing him again after all these years. The jet-black hair, square determined jaw, and cheekbones sculpted from granite looked even better than she remembered. The tall, muscular body she remembered running her hands over way too many times. And blue eyes that could mesmerize and captivate with just a glance as he was doing to her now.

Except that when she knew him he was simply plain old Nicholas Carter, not Prince Nicholas Corsairs, heir to some throne in a place she'd never heard of and at the moment didn't care to figure out. He was the same man who had left her standing alone in their apartment ten years prior with nothing more than a quick kiss and a goodbye as he walked out the door never to return until now. The same man who haunted her dreams nearly every night. And the same man Isabelle thought she'd never have to see again.

And yet here Nicholas was standing before her. Confusion sparred with the anger she was presently experiencing at the two men's sudden appearance in the surgical suite. The words she wanted to say stuck in her throat and all Isabelle could do was stare at Nicholas in silence. She cursed herself for her inability to formulate a retort. Words never failed her and today should have been no different. But something about seeing the man brought back all the feelings she'd pushed to the bottom of her heart.

She squared her shoulders and swung her gaze back to Kevin. "Regardless, is there a specific reason it couldn't have waited until I was out of surgery?"

Kevin nodded. "Yes and no."

Isabelle kept a tight grip on her temper. She knew Kevin wouldn't have done it without a good reason. But seeing who his guest was chased all rational behavior from her mind. Throughout the years, Kevin had been a trusted friend, but more so a mentor. After his near fatal accident, he was forced to stop performing surgery and had taken it upon himself to make Isabelle his protégé. Under his tutelage, she had accomplished more than she ever could have hoped to on her own. For that fact alone, she owed him the courtesy of listening to his explanation.

"I don't understand; which is it, Kevin?" Isabelle pointedly stared at the clock on the wall. "I have three more procedures to attend to and I don't like to keep my patients waiting. Unless this is an emergency, I trust the matter can wait until I've finished," she declared, effectively ending the discussion.

"Doctor Tandori, I have no wish to cause you delays with your procedures. Pardon the untimely intrusion of my visit. I was under the impression you knew I would be touring the hospital facility today. We will talk when you are through with your patients. I'll meet you in Doctor Aldridge's office upon completion of the procedures. In fact, I very much look forward to it." Nicholas inclined his head in her direction.

Isabelle eyed him warily, furious that her pulse was still racing out of control. What was Nicholas up to? And why would she have known he was at the hospital? Other than the fact she now realized he was the visitor Eleanor had spoken of earlier, nothing was making sense. More importantly, whatever it was would have to wait until after her day was finished. He was the least of her concerns for the time being; at least that's what Isabelle tried to tell herself.

"Fine. Until then, Prince Corsairs." Isabelle made a concerted effort to keep her voice neutral as she pushed through the swinging doors and walked out of the room without a backward glance at either man.

*

Nicholas tried to pay attention to what the chief of staff was telling him, but his mind kept drifting back to Isabelle. A look akin to panic flitted through her gaze when she saw him in the surgical suite, then quickly masked her expression. The other man may not have seen it, but Nicholas most certainly did. She'd known exactly who he was from the second their eyes met and she didn't look the least bit pleased to see him.

Seeing her again brought about a reaction in Nicholas he hadn't expected. When she turned her full attention on him, it was as if the rest of the room faded away. Surprise flickered in her eyes, but was quickly replaced by indifference. She looked amazing. The passing years only enhanced her features, bringing to light the successful woman in the surgical scrubs that managed quite nicely since his abrupt departure from her life.

He shot a sideways glance at the man walking down the hallway next to him. It was obvious Kevin Aldridge and Isabelle knew each other well. But how well, Nicholas wondered. He tamped down the notion they might be lovers or were in the past. Not that any of it mattered to him. They'd both moved on with their lives during their time apart. Why the thought even popped into his head, Nicholas wasn't sure. He knew that before the day had ended, he would know the answer despite his own reservations.

"I must say Doctor Tandori is an excellent choice. Her record, as you know, is exemplary. She's been an asset to the hospital since the day she finished her residency. In fact, it was upon my recommendation she was considered for the position in cardiology."

"Very impressive," Nicholas murmured. Doctor Aldridge continued to reel off a quite sizeable list of Isabelle's many attributes, but Nicholas's thoughts were occupied elsewhere.

"You've got quite a record yourself if you don't mind my saying so, Your Highness. The hospital on Wellfleet Isle was quite an undertaking from what I've read."

Nicholas brushed off the compliment with a wave of his hand. The last thing he wanted to do was discuss his own credentials. But Kevin Aldridge had obviously done his homework on Nicholas as well, leveling the playing field in regard to why Nicholas was here. "I assure you my accomplishments pale in comparison to those of Doctor Tandori."

Accomplishments Nicholas hoped would carry over into his father's care. Though "hoped" would be the wrong word to use. Given her track record, Nicholas was positive Isabelle taking over his father's case would make a significant difference to his father's recovery.

Doctor Aldridge stopped walking and Nicholas came to an abrupt halt rather than plow into the man.

"Ah, I see Doctor Tandori is out of surgery now."

Nicholas followed his gaze and saw Isabelle talking with a young woman in a wheelchair farther down the hallway of the Cardiac

Care Department. Intent on her conversation, Nicholas took the opportunity to study her. The newspaper clippings and medical journal articles he read didn't do her justice. The Isabelle he knew was young, carefree, and out to change the world. The one before him now had matured into a stunning woman. She knew what she wanted and was not afraid to go after it. Had it not been for her surgical team standing at the ready, Nicholas harbored no doubt both he and Doctor Aldridge would have gotten a severe dressing down. One they deserved in relation to their untimely intrusion during a surgical procedure. If it had been him, Nicholas knew he wouldn't have tempered his outburst in the least.

Her auburn hair was longer, falling in loose curls about her shoulders, not the short bob she wore back in college. Dark lashes framed expressive brown eyes flecked with gold. Petite in stature, the top of her head barely reached his chin, but Nicholas knew she was a formidable foe when angered. He recalled the times he would cajole her from that same anger with kisses. What drew his attention now was her body. Despite how Isabelle tried to cover up her womanly curves beneath the loose fitting lab coat, she oozed sex appeal that caught him right in the solar plexus.

Nicholas was surprised at the depth of emotions his body experienced at seeing her again. The itch to run his fingers through her hair had him clenching his hands into fists at his side. He wanted to tip her head back and stare into those eyes, losing himself in their expressive brown depths. Even now just thinking about her brought about a tug of arousal so swift it nearly brought him to his knees.

Ten years had done nothing to quell the instant reaction his body had to hers. The husky sound of her laughter drifted down the hallway, washing over him, bringing back unbidden memories of other times. Times shrouded in darkness, where two bodies became one under the guise of night. They'd taught one another the ways of love, how to give and receive pleasure, learning what each preferred, and brought about the satisfaction they sought. His lower body tightened as the memories assailed him. Maybe this wasn't the best idea, Nicholas mentally chastised himself, but it was the only option he had left. And Nicholas was damned sure he was going to avail himself of it.

He watched as she leaned over and enveloped the young woman in a tight hug. Nicholas heard her words of thanks as Isabelle brushed aside the comments, putting the praise firmly back upon the young woman as was warranted. A second later, Isabelle lifted her head as though sensing his presence, turned, and caught his stare. Her smile faded, to be quickly replaced by wariness. She patted the woman's hand before moving back toward the reception desk.

He had been summarily dismissed with only a glance.

Could it be Isabelle was just as affected as he by his unexpected appearance in her life? It was another riddle for Nicholas to unravel regarding the beautiful woman down the corridor. He smiled to himself, suppressing a chuckle. If she thought he would fade into the woodwork that easily, then Doctor Isabelle Tandori had another thing coming.

Chapter Two

"Isabelle, this isn't just some guy we're talking about here. This is His Royal Highness Nicholas Demeter Corsairs, heir to the throne of Wellfleet Isle and he requests the honor of your presence. He wants you to take over the care of his father, who is at present ill with a serious heart condition. Isabelle, he wants *you*. I don't know if you realize this or not, but it's a great honor to be handpicked by someone of his stature. Do you realize the clout this man has? Most doctors would give their right arm to be asked to do this. Why are you fighting so hard not to say yes?"

Isabelle shook her head. She wasn't about to reveal the past she shared with Nicholas. That was no one's business except her own. All afternoon Nicholas filled her thoughts, occupied her mind. The man was a prince and Isabelle knew she should have been stunned by the news, but somehow she wasn't. What bothered her even more was the fact he was here in her hospital, in her surgical suite, and he needed her to help him.

"Kevin, as flattered as I am by the offer, my work is here, my life is here, and my home is here. I'm sure there must be someone else who can fill the position Nicho...the prince is offering."

"Somehow flattered is not the word I'd have chosen to describe your lack of enthusiasm. But apparently, you're the name at the top of their list. And need I remind you it would reflect quite favorably on the hospital if you were to accept the position."

Isabelle sighed, knowing this conversation was far from over. She opened her mouth to protest but Kevin cut her off.

"Just hear me out first. For whatever reason and I suspect you have a very good idea, the man wants you. Look Isabelle, I'm not asking you to divulge anything that happened between you and the prince. Your relationship is none of my concern. But this position could propel your career forward in ways you've never even dreamt of. You'd be in the catbird seat to secure grants and backing for whatever your heart desired in the field of cardiology. The position is only for six months. Take some time to mull it over. Can you do that much for me?"

Her fingers clenched at the soft fabric on the arm of the chair. She didn't want to think about the offer, she wanted to refuse and get back to her job. But Isabelle knew it wouldn't be that simple. She knew how hard it was to get a grant approved. Heaven knows she'd completed her fair share of the paperwork in the past. She'd jumped through hoops, justified the needs, and done everything but raise the money herself. But this was Nicholas that Kevin was talking about. The man who'd broken her heart and left her when she'd needed him most.

Kevin shifted his gaze as he picked up a pen from the desk and toyed with it, rolling it back and forth between his fingers. When he next spoke, his voice was more moderated than before. "Look, we both know this is an unusual set of circumstances. I'm your friend but I'm also your employer. I have to watch out for everyone's best interests and right now the hospital is about to become the recipient of an incredibly large, almost to the point of obscene donation if you say yes. All you have to do is sign on the dotted line to make it official. Do I have to spell out for you what that means in this economy?"

"And if I refuse the offer?" Isabelle could hear where this was going. Money was a big motivator, but publicity was an even bigger draw.

"The hospital and I hope that won't be an issue." His voice tight, Kevin neatly avoided her eyes. "You've been an asset to this hospital since the day you were hired in and we…the board feels this would be a tremendous opportunity for not only you, but the entire Cardiac Care Department as well."

Her stomach plummeted. "That's low even for you, Kevin. So I take it this is emotional blackmail?"

"No, it's business."

His barb hit home. Suddenly, everything became clear. Whatever decision the hospital made regarding the way Isabelle answered, Kevin would wholeheartedly enforce whether he wanted to or not because it was his job to do so.

For a second, Isabel felt sick to her stomach. Then her temper flared as she contemplated her options, the anger rolled through her veins even as she tried to deflect it. Her choices were limited to a simple yes or no. By saying yes, the hospital would benefit greatly from the money and publicity Nicholas offered. If she said no, Isabelle didn't want to think about what the hospital would do. The wrong decision could quite possibly bring about the end of her career at Garner General. She closed her eyes and sucked in a shaky breath, thinking about all the hard work she'd accomplished over the years. Either way the odds were stacked quite neatly against her.

*

Following the secretary's instructions to the letter, Nicholas knocked on the outer door of Kevin Aldridge's office and waited. Just a few minutes before, he'd seen Isabelle enter and close the door behind her. He wondered what they were discussing. Not that any of it was his business, except for the matter at hand. Then it most certainly involved him.

"Come in," Kevin called out from the other side.

Nicholas turned the knob, pushed open the door, and stepped into the room. The palpable tension between the two occupants was instantly obvious. "Am I interrupting? I could return later if you haven't finished conducting your business. Whatever you would prefer, Doctor Aldridge?"

Kevin rose from his seat behind the desk. "No, that's not necessary. Please have a seat. We were discussing your more than generous offer of employment regarding Doctor Tandori."

Nicholas moved forward and took the chair next to Isabelle, who sat with her arms crossed tightly across her chest, her toe tapping the carpeted floor in a muted staccato beat. She ignored him as pointedly as she could manage and the notion made Nicholas want to smile. But he wisely did not allow himself to engage in the action.

"Somehow I have the distinct impression Doctor Tandori does not share your enthusiasm."

She swung to face him and Nicholas didn't need to meet her heated stare to know she was furious. The waves of anger emanated off her from the second he'd reappeared in her life. "If looks could kill" was the phrase that popped immediately to his mind. Granted, their parting had been abrupt ten years prior, but hadn't Nicholas made sure she was taken care of in his absence? That her life would go on in the same manner it had been? Why the blatant hostility toward him even now?

"Would you mind giving us a few minutes alone, Doctor Aldridge?" Nicholas directed his question to Kevin, but his gaze never left Isabelle's face. "I wish to speak to Doctor Tandori in private if you have no objections."

Kevin looked at Nicholas, then back to Isabelle, uncertainty on his face as he pondered leaving them alone. With a quick shrug of his shoulder, he conceded to Nicholas's wishes. "Certainly, I'll check back in with you later. Please notify my secretary if you need anything." He closed the door behind him.

Nicholas mentally counted to ten, waiting for Isabelle's outburst. As expected, he didn't have long to wait before she rounded on him, her auburn curls swinging softly about her shoulders.

"What do you think you're doing coming here like this?" Her hands now braced on the arms of the chair as she confronted him.

Nicholas lifted his shoulders nonchalantly in response, refusing to rise to the bait. "Coming here like what? I came to engage your services as a physician for my father, the King of Wellfleet Isle."

"There must be dozens of other candidates that are as equally suited to handle this responsibility. Why not choose one of them instead?"

"The techniques you've pioneered for artery replacement surgery are exemplary. You are well respected by your colleagues and this hospital. And as such, you have been found to be the perfect choice to prepare my father for his surgery. That is the reason why I chose you." What he didn't say was she was the only surgeon that came to his mind and the only one he couldn't get out of his mind. If other doctors' qualifications were as exemplary as Isabelle's, Nicholas hadn't bothered to pursue checking out their references. She was the one he wanted in more ways than one.

"Well, bully for me. Doesn't your father already have a royal physician to attend to his care? Someone who can assist him right up until the day of surgery and then with his convalescence?"

"Not anymore. The man was dismissed this morning." Now it was Nicholas's turn to look away.

"What aren't you telling me about this case, Nicholas?"

"My father hasn't actually agreed to the heart transplant, but he will. With your guidance, he will see it is necessary. Without it, he may not live another year."

"So you expect me to 'make' him say yes? You have got to be kidding me."

Nicholas held up his hand in an effort to stop her from arguing. "This is not up for discussion any further, Isabelle. I have already made my decision and it is final."

"This isn't your decision to make. It's mine as well." She pressed on as Nicholas expected.

Nicholas sighed and pinched the bridge of his nose. "My time is limited and I would prefer not to spend the rest of this afternoon arguing with you over mundane details."

"And mine isn't? I have a full-time job that requires my attention here in this hospital, patients I see on a regular basis, and private commitments outside of the hospital."

Nicholas shook his head. "No, not anymore you don't."

"Excuse me? What do you mean by that?" She stood up, hands now firmly planted on her hips.

"After I sought you out, I took the liberty of conferring with your employer in regard to your present work load. As of today, right now actually," Nicholas looked down at his watch to confirm the time. "You are on an extended six-month leave of absence."

"You had no right to do that." Isabelle paced the confines of Doctor Aldridge's office, her steps tight and terse, and disbelief marring her features.

Nicholas rose to his feet, towering a good six inches over her, his gaze narrowed on her face, his voice low and controlled. "I had every right. I am the future King of Wellfleet Isle."

"Not to me, you're not. To me, you're a tyrant and a bully who believes his word is law and he can boss people around at will." Her words were punctuated by the jab of her index finger against his breastbone with every other word. When she finished, Isabelle turned on her heel and left Kevin's office, slamming the door behind her.

"Well, all in all that went remarkably well. Possibly better than even I expected it would."

Nicholas closed his eyes and sat back down. A hint of lavender invaded his senses and he realized it was the lingering scent of Isabelle's perfume. A smile tugged at his lips as he remembered her stating a long time ago that the aroma of lavender was a calming influence to her soul. Some things never changed and for that one small fact he should be grateful.

He could still feel the press of her long, slender finger to his chest, the sensation not altogether unpleasant or unwelcome, just there. Nicholas sat quietly for a few minutes reliving their conversation, and let out a long low breath. At least Isabelle didn't refuse his offer outright. It was a small step in the right direction. Reaching into his pocket, Nicholas withdrew his cell phone, punched in a quick set of numbers, then waited for the call to be answered.

"Good afternoon, Denton. How's Father doing today?"

Nicholas listened to the ensuing answer from the private care nurse for his father. "That's very encouraging news. Please make sure Father continues on with his oxygen as we've discussed. I've met with a snag on this end and my departure from the States will be delayed a day." He paused. "No, nothing I can't handle. Just a small glitch in my travel arrangements. Tell Father I'll see him soon and I'll call when en route."

Nicholas slipped the phone into the pocket of his suit coat, rose from the chair and went in search of Isabelle. He wasn't there when his mother became ill and died suddenly, but Nicholas knew he would do everything in his power to make sure his father had the best care possible and right now, that meant Doctor Isabelle Tandori. Whether she knew it or not, she was going to return with him to Wellfleet Isle.

*

Isabelle shut the front door of her condo and leaned back against it, letting the welcoming silence of her home wrap itself around her. She drew in a deep breath, and then exhaled slowly. Today had been quite an adventure, and one she hadn't expected. Never one to run from a fight, right now all she wanted was to crawl into her bed, pull the covers over her head, and forget the world existed.

Yet, it would change nothing. Nicholas was here in the States and, short of famine, fire, or flood, he wasn't leaving until she accepted the job offer. She knew from prior experience, he'd never been good at taking no for an answer. He would dig in his heels and wait out his opponent. But if he thought she was going to smile sweetly and acquiesce, the man had another thing coming.

Isabelle dropped her briefcase and keys on the kitchen table and glanced over at the morning's newspaper on the counter. A picture of Nicholas and the board of directors at Garner General Hospital covered most of the front page. The last thing she wanted was to think about the man, but out of curiosity, Isabelle picked up the paper and read the piece. Minutes later, she plopped down heavily on the sofa, tossed the paper aside, and buried her face in her hands.

The amount of money Nicholas donated to the hospital was astronomical, to the point of obscene being an understatement. All to ensure she would return to Wellfleet Isle and care for his ailing father. Granted, that part was left out of the story for which Isabelle was eternally grateful. But what the article did include was the fact that she was the doctor chosen to go to Wellfleet Isle. She was the one leaving her current position at Garner General Hospital in order to go care for the king. And at the moment, she was the one who had yet to accept the offer. By now, her parents would be aware of the article as well. They would be so pleased if their daughter made the right decision. A decision based on outward appearances, as opposed to doing the right thing for the right reasons.

Would they be concerned for their only child flying off to some unknown island nation escorted by a prince to care for a king? No, instead they'd be touting the news to their friends of her newly acquired status as the royal physician. Never once would they inquire if Isabelle were happy. Never once would they care enough to ask their daughter if they could help her through the difficult decision making process. Not that she would have given them any opportunity to help her decide her own fate. They would have pushed her into saying yes because it would elevate their social status greatly, something Isabelle didn't give a hoot about. This decision was to be hers alone.

She'd made it through the last ten years of her life managing quite nicely on her own. Right up until today, when Prince Nicholas Corsair walked into her surgical suite, disrupting her entire world. Even now the memory of his leaving was as clear as the day it happened. She'd been devastated over his departure, devastated over the miscarriage, and devastated all her hopes and dreams had been shattered in one fell swoop. Now when she'd finally gotten her life where she wanted it, he walked back through the door and into her thoughts.

Isabelle closed her eyes and fought down the flush of heat that swept over her at the mere thought of the man. Fanning her hands in front of her face did nothing to diffuse the situation, nor tame the fire that burned inside her at seeing Nicholas again.

The last thing she wanted or needed was Nicholas back in her life, but if she refused, the fallout from the lost money would be enormous. Kevin made his feelings clear and Isabelle hesitated to even think of the hospital's position if she refused. Suck it up and get on with it.

Isabelle was always concise, methodical, and almost anal in her thought process. Her personal and professional life both deserved the same thorough consideration. If this was any other circumstance and someone needed, no make that *demanded*, an immediate answer from her, Isabelle knew she would have automatically said no. That's just the way it was, which was why the decision was currently tearing her apart. She literally had no time to debate the pros or cons of the situation in the manner she normally afforded herself. Worse yet at this point she'd virtually no option for refusal without causing an international incident.

The problem with saying yes to Nicholas unearthed memories from the past she preferred remained buried in the deep, dark recesses of her mind. Her cell phone rang and Isabelle walked into the kitchen to retrieve it. The screen flashed "private number" and she was half tempted not to answer, but knew it could be the hospital with an emergency.

"Hello."

"Good evening Isabelle. I trust your ride home was uneventful since I was unable to reconnect with you before your departure from the hospital this afternoon."

The sound of his rich, deep voice filtered through the receiver, tickling her senses, wrapping itself around her like a lover's embrace. It took Isabelle a few seconds before she found her voice.

"Nicholas, how did you get my number?"

"I have my ways."

Isabelle imagined he'd gotten it from Kevin Aldridge. He'd probably given Nicholas her address in order to sway her to accept the position. She wouldn't be surprised if he'd told the man where she hid her spare key.

"I believe we have some unfinished business. Shall we conduct it on the telephone, or would you prefer I come to your home?"

"No." Panicked, Isabelle swung around and inadvertently caught the stack of medical books on the kitchen table with her elbow. They crashed to the floor with a resounding thud. Trying to slow her racing heartbeat, she closed her eyes and fought for calm. The last thing she wanted was Nicholas to come here. Being alone with him in her home would play havoc on her nerves, and she needed her wits about her. "No, over the phone will be fine."

"Is everything all right?"

"Everything's fine, just peachy keen wonderful," Isabelle muttered as she bent to retrieve the books from the floor.

She heard him chuckle at her frustrated response, causing her body to go into a bone melting, knees quivering, sweaty palms reaction she couldn't fight off. The last thing she needed was to feel nervous around Nicholas. Truth was she didn't want to feel anything at all, but couldn't help herself.

"I assume by now you've seen the article in today's paper?"

"Yes, I have." She glanced at the newspaper on the coffee table. "That was a very nice preemptive move on the part of the hospital putting it in the paper ahead of time. I'm guessing that was done on purpose. Kudos to whoever thought it up. Makes it quite difficult for me to refuse, doesn't it?"

"If memory serves, I don't believe we covered what you would receive for your services as my father's personal physician. I will triple your salary as well as make a sizeable donation to the charity of your choice in return for the interruption of your life."

"Really, how sizeable?" Isabelle asked. Tripling her salary was a nice coup. Adding in a big donation on top of that would be icing on the cake if she were to accept the job.

He mentioned a dollar figure that was almost beyond belief and Isabelle reached to steady herself against the kitchen counter. The man had more money than was humanly possible, it seemed. Her fingers tightened on the cell phone for fear she might drop it. The kind of money he offered would go a long way to provide care and much needed supplies to any of the half dozen organizations she currently supported. Nicholas was making it harder to refuse his offer with every passing second. And somehow Isabelle didn't doubt he knew exactly what he was doing.

"My staff has made all the arrangements for your condo as well. Your mail will be forwarded in your absence, and the rent and utilities will be paid until your return. A property management company will take care of any issues that arise in your absence. I apologize in advance for any inconvenience this might cause."

A shard of pain shot through Isabelle as his familiar words hit home. Did he really think his apology would mean any more to her now? Calling it an inconvenience was an understatement in the grand scheme of things. Nicholas expected her to turn her life upside down because he wanted her as his father's physician. If this was what it would be like to be at the beck and call of a royal family, Isabelle wasn't sure she wanted any part of it.

"A car will pick you up at eight-thirty tomorrow morning and drive you to the airport. I'll meet you aboard the private plane. Please feel free to pack whatever you deem necessary for the immediate present. Whatever else you require will be shipped to you within the next two weeks. If a need arises for anything else, it will be provided while you are on Wellfleet Isle. You have only but to ask."

Isabelle pulled her disjointed thoughts back to the conversation. "You're presuming an awful lot right now, aren't you, Nicholas? I haven't officially agreed to your offer. You do realize that?"

He continued on as if she hadn't said a word. "I suggest you be ready when the driver arrives at your door."

"Or else?"

"I shall toss you over my shoulder and carry you to the car in full view of your neighbors. It makes no difference to me." The timbre of his voice dropped lower and a shiver skittered down her spine.

"Really, Nicholas, are you sure you want to tempt fate a second time?" The minute the words left her mouth, Isabelle had no doubt he would do exactly that.

She closed her eyes, recalling a time the caveman routine worked just as he'd stated, and she and Nicholas ended up spending the afternoon and most of the evening in bed.

Isabelle knew what she had to do. Once she agreed to his demands—no, make that his *incredibly hard to refuse job offer*—there would be no turning back. "Fine, you win. I'll go to Wellfleet Isle with you and be your father's doctor. And I'll be ready when the driver gets here in the morning."

"Thank you, Isabelle, I look forward to seeing you tomorrow."

But would she be ready to face Nicholas? To spend the next six months living in close proximity with the man? Now she would be under the same roof as him. For three years, she'd spent every day and every night with the man. Slept next to him in the same bed, planned their future together in the darkness of the night into the wee hours of the morning, and loved him beyond words. Her stomach gave a sickening lurch as Isabelle remembered his whispered promises of their life together after med school and residency. Of the life they would create, the family they would raise, the…

The memories washed over her and Isabelle lifted her hand to her mouth to stifle the sob.

She wouldn't let him back into her heart. What kind of person walked away without a backwards glance at someone they professed to love? The kind that haunted her dreams at night, leaving her wanting more come the light of day.

This would never do, Isabelle told herself. It was just a job. A temporary position no less, she reminded herself after hanging up the phone. After six months, she could return to her old job and resume her life here in the States. A life that didn't include His Highness Nicholas Corsairs, heir to the throne of Wellfleet Isle.

Isabelle walked into the bathroom, turned on the bathtub faucet, and then added a handful of bath salts. What she needed was a chance to relax before her brain exploded. She dropped her clothes on the tile floor, stepped into the tub, and lowered herself down slowly into the hot, lavender-scented bath water. She closed her eyes and sighed, letting the hot water seep into her frazzled nerves. If this were a normal night, she'd have brought a glass of wine into the bathroom with her, turned on some Michael Buble, and tuned out the world. Then again, as of late, she could count the normal nights on one hand. Nights when she hit her bed before three in the morning, fell into a restless sleep, and was ready to start all over again before the sun rose the next morning. But this was not normal in any sense of the word, and right now a glass of wine would only confuse matters.

Tomorrow she'd be flying half a million miles across the country to a place she knew nothing about, to care for a man who barely knew her. Jerking herself upright, Isabelle grabbed the side of the tub, her erratic motions splashing sudsy water over the edge and onto the bathmat. What if she wasn't a virtual stranger to the king? What if the king knew more than just the fact she and Nicholas had lived together. What if he knew about everything?

Isabelle shook her head and sunk back into the fragrant bubbles. No, it wasn't possible. No one knew about the past. About the night that Nicholas left the apartment, returned to his family, and left her alone. And no one ever would. She was worrying herself into a panic over nothing. If anyone had known, they would have said so by now. She had to believe they would have.

After the miscarriage, when she tried to contact him, his cell phone had been disconnected. She'd gone to the admissions office of the college and asked for his address, but they wouldn't give out any personal information regarding a student. Against policy, they told her. She even looked online for him and found no information on a Nicholas Carter attending medical school. It was as if all traces of Nicholas disappeared from the apartment and her life the day he walked out.

Looking back, it seemed odd she'd never questioned Nicholas more about his family during the time they'd lived together. When she asked where he lived, he would only say his family was far away, and then quickly drop the subject. She was so much in love with him it didn't matter. Or at least she thought she'd been in love. But love didn't leave you standing alone in the dark fighting for your unborn baby's life. Now, Isabelle could have kicked herself for her stupidity.

With a heavy heart, she climbed from the tub, dried herself off and pulled on her favorite cotton pajamas. It was time to begin the task of leaving behind her old life. What to pack now and what to send for later? Having to choose was quite a dilemma.

In the end, Isabelle packed as though she were going on a long vacation and took her chances that the rest would fall into place.

When she finished, her suitcases were stacked inside the foyer by the front door. She walked through her condo one final time, running her fingers over the back of the comfy, brown leather sofa, lingering for a last glance out the large living room window at the multicolored lights of the city. Her vision clouded as the sheen of tears filled her eyes. She swiped them away with the back of her hand before turning out the lights and heading down the hall.

Once in her bedroom, she lifted the shell-covered jewelry box from her dresser and sat it on the bed in front of her. Opening the lid, she lifted out the small square of white paper, carefully unfolding it until it lay flat on the bed before her. The words typed in bold letters across the first line of the page caught her attention immediately.

Congratulations, your pregnancy test is positive!

Closing her eyes tightly, Isabelle placed her palm across the paper, blotting out the rest of the words. She didn't need to read the letter to know what it said. Over the years, every word was ingrained in her mind, imprinted on her soul. Folding the paper and returning it to the box, she replaced it on the dresser. There was no reason to bring that along with her to Wellfleet Isle. Some memories were better left forgotten.

*

Staring out the picture window at the lights of the city, Nicholas swirled the amber liquid in the tumbler before taking a drink. Granted it was only a place to lay his head, yet he hated the impersonal feel of the bland beige colors of the hotel room walls and longed for the serenity of the palace and his suite of rooms. The alcohol burned and soothed his spirits as it slid down his throat, warming his insides, filling up the empty places. Isabelle accepted the offer to be his father's physician. Until this moment, Nicholas wasn't aware how much her acceptance meant to him. It was as though a huge weight had been lifted when she told him yes. Now, the matter was settled and he could get back to the palace and tend to business as usual.

Watching her in the operating room earlier in the day brought the realization of how long it had been since he performed a surgery. Too long, Nicholas thought. Quite possibly right before news of his mother's passing reached him. Right before he'd left to go home and resume his place and position in the royal family. And right before he'd walked out the door of their apartment and left Isabelle looking after him with such disappointment on her face. A look he'd never forgotten, even after all this time.

The scent of her perfume wrapped itself around him, even now as the airy wisp of lavender still burned into his brain. Every time he'd come in contact with the fragrance over the years, he'd thought of Isabelle. Missing her, needing her, wanting her, but not knowing how to go back and change what happened with his leaving. She was the one person who never needed more from him than he was willing to give. She had given herself freely to the man she thought he was, the fake persona he'd built for himself, surrounded himself with in order to escape media attention and favoritism in exchange for his freedom.

If he'd been any kind of man, he would have told her the truth from the onset. But no, instead Nicholas kept his true identity hidden, allowing Isabelle to believe he was Nicholas Carter, a medical student studying for his degree the same as she. Isabelle had been his rock, his life, and more importantly, his lover during their three years together. She loved him for who he was, not as a royal. She'd believed in him, never doubted that he would one day become a great doctor.

Nicholas gave a derisive snort. She had become the great doctor, not he. He had become... What had he become? The next in line for the throne of Wellfleet Isle. A man not in charge of his own destiny, but definitely in charge of the people of a small island country. Son to a ruler who was now fighting for his life. And a man who walked away from the best thing that ever happened to him ten years ago.

He downed the rest of the liquid in two swallows, and then set the glass on the table next to his half-eaten supper. Tomorrow they would be en route to Wellfleet Isle and everything would once again be all right. It had to be, Nicholas thought. He wouldn't lose another parent. Having Isabelle there would see to that.

Isabelle.

Nicholas wondered what she was doing at that exact moment. A few quite erotic images filled his head as he tried to shake off the notion. No, this would never do. He needed to keep his mind focused firmly on her caring for his father and not on what she could do for him.

His cell phone rang and Nicholas glanced down at the number. He scowled as he lifted the phone to his ear.

"Hello."

"Hello, Nicholas. I wondered whether you would be receptive to my call."

"Aidan, it's been a while since we've spoken. To what do I owe the pleasure?" Nicholas reached for the glass, and then remembered he'd finished the Scotch. Pity the glass wasn't full at present. He'd have liked to indulge himself; especially after the conversation he was about to have.

"Never one to mince words, were you big brother? I'll make this short and sweet. I'm coming back to Wellfleet Isle within the month. We need to talk."

No "How's Father doing?" or "Are you well?" Just another cryptic statement from a brother he hadn't seen in over five years. Nicholas fought down the urge to throw something across the room, but restrained himself from the gesture. The last thing he wanted was to talk to Aidan, the "Playboy Prince," as the people of Wellfleet Isle dubbed him. Nicholas cleaned up enough of his younger brother's messes, kept the news from the papers, and isolated the king from the fallout that did occur when all was said and done and Aidan breezed off to his next pursuit. But for the sake of their father, Nicholas would tamp down his own anger and resentment in order to keep peace within the royal family. It was time his brother stepped up and learned to resolve his own problems. Nicholas had enough to keep him occupied for a fair amount of time: a slender auburn-haired woman with expressive brown eyes that could bring him to his knees with merely a touch.

Chapter Three

Nicholas sat in the limousine nursing a self-induced headache. He'd finished off the remaining contents of a bottle of Scotch after talking to his brother the previous night. Yet the alcohol had nothing to do with the way he felt. Instead it was the dreams that filled his head from the moment he closed his eyes. Dreams of Isabelle, dreams of the two of them together, and dreams of things better left to the imagination. Of which his had certainly run overtime. He tried to ignore the warning bells clanging in his head, but couldn't. Sleep was a long time coming as Nicholas warred between his duty to his people and the longing in his limbs for Isabelle.

Duty must always come first, he told himself. His people were top priority, yet... With one glance at Isabelle, Wellfleet Isle faded to the back of his mind. Nicholas turned his gaze to the window and watched intently as the driver loaded Isabelle's luggage onto the royal family's private jet while she remained seated inside the other limousine. She'd shown up as promised, arriving on time, if not early. While he couldn't see clearly through the tinted windows, Nicholas knew Isabelle was nervous. As much as she pretended otherwise in the past, Isabelle was very comfortable in her surroundings as long as they didn't change. She liked to keep things familiar and constant. A set schedule followed by a set routine, day in and day out.

She'd agreed to his offer of employment, even if it came with quite a few strings attached. Regardless, Nicholas knew he would have found a way to convince her should she have refused, even if it meant driving over to her home in the middle of the night. He chuckled at the memory of her sounding so frantic on the telephone when he suggested stopping by. The panic in her voice at the thought of him showing up on her doorstep, though he would have welcomed the opportunity to see her home. And it would have given him a chance to see if she retained anything of their past life together. Why the idea even came to mind Nicholas wasn't sure.

It would be nice to have her on the island, give him the opportunity to show her his home.

His home.

At one time, their apartment back in Maryland had been his home. No, make that their home. A home they created together. Weekends spent sleeping in, making love, then scouring the flea markets and consignment shops in hopes of snagging that special something. Nicholas recalled their double bed. Isabelle had seen the metal headboard discarded at the curb and convinced Nicholas to bring it home. To hand carry it over ten blocks and across many busy streets as he remembered. The bed served them well, both day and night.

Now a groan escaped his lips and Nicholas tamped down the inciting fire in his groin. Everything about Isabelle brought memories whether he wanted them or not. Yet he knew he would cherish every single one. But that was all they could be, for royalty did not engage in a dalliance with an outsider. The last thing he wanted or needed was another scandal dirtying his hands. With a quick glance at his watch, Nicholas saw it was time to depart.

A movement outside the window caught his attention and he watched Isabelle alight from the limo and head toward the jet. Her leather jacket seemed ill-equipped for the brutal Chicago weather, but in a matter of a few hours the garment would no longer be necessary. The temperatures on Wellfleet Isle had reached a pleasant 72 degrees per the weather report Nicholas read.

Regardless, Nicholas knew the contours of her body like the back of his hand. Though now they were of a grown woman of thirty-two, not a teenager anymore. The passage of time only enhanced her beauty. If Isabelle thought she was concealing her curves under her white lab coat or even loose surgical scrubs, then she was sorely mistaken as every inch of her screamed pure sexual, sensual woman. Any man in his right mind would notice them post haste.

The thought of other men noticing her curves bothered him and Nicholas frowned at the realization. He had no claims on Isabelle at present, regardless of what his body was telling him.

Nicholas wiped his hands down the side of his pants. His palms were sweaty and it was difficult to believe he was experiencing such a juvenile reaction. Nicholas prided himself on his composure, yet at the moment was feeling anything but.

He rapped his knuckles against the window and the driver immediately opened the door, flooding the interior of the limo with sunlight. Nicholas exited the vehicle and headed for the jet. At the top of the stairs, he looked out over the tarmac, surveying the view. It had been a long time since his last trip to the States and it would be even longer before he returned. It was time to put his plan into motion. The sooner they got back to Wellfleet Isle and his father, the better.

Heading straight toward the cockpit, Nicholas conferred with the pilot and copilot regarding the flight plan previously filed; then walked to his seat and settled in. Once clearance had been received from the tower, they'd be on their way. Fastening his seatbelt across his lap, he ventured a glance at Isabelle.

She sat quietly across the aisle, seatbelt secure, fingers tapping out an erratic rhythm on the arms of the leather seat as her gaze was focused forward. Flying had never been her strong suit; Nicholas remembered. She preferred driving, regardless of the length of the trip, and keeping her feet firmly on the ground. As much as she relished the idea of getting from one place to another in a matter of a few short hours, take-off and landing never failed to set her nerves to a panicked frenzy. Today appeared to be no exception. Her very expressive body language said it all.

Nicholas felt the vibration of the engines as the plane readied for take-off. Hoping to cajole her out of her rising apprehension, he leaned across the aisle and took her clammy hand in his, nearly prying it from the arm of the chair and wrapping his fingers around hers.

"If you'd like, I could come sit next to you and hold your hand. Would that soothe your fears?" He stroked his thumb over the inside of her wrist, feeling the erratic beat of her pulse beneath his finger.

Isabelle quickly snatched her hand back and laced her fingers together in her lap. A quite becoming flush of pink rose to her cheeks as she gaped at him, then quickly closed her mouth and shook her head. "No, no thank you. I'll be fine once we're in the air."

"I find it helps if you concentrate on something else. Focus your attention elsewhere, a magazine perhaps," he offered.

"I know it doesn't make any sense to be so fearful of flying."

"If it does to you, then that is all that matters."

Nicholas watched the way Isabelle renewed her attack on the armrests, her knuckles a stark white against the burgundy leather. She closed her eyes and gnawed on her lower lip as Nicholas fought down the urge to smooth his finger across her mouth, touch her very kissable lips and tell her everything would be all right. But he couldn't and he didn't. Nicholas squirmed in his seat, the front of his trousers now too tight for comfort. He shifted his stance to no avail.

As the plane rose into the air, Nicholas released his seatbelt and moved across the aisle to where Isabelle sat, her head resting on the seat back, eyes closed. Settling himself on the bench seat next to her, he folded his arms across his chest and studied her.

A smile crossed his face at the memory of how she looked

back then, waking up in his arms each morning in their tiny one-bedroom apartment, his fingers tangled in her auburn curls, their legs intertwined, their naked bodies pressed close together. Her expressive brown eyes still clouded with sleep, she would turn in his arms to kiss him and whisper good morning, caressing him boldly under the covers, wrapping her body around him, welcoming him into her body. His groin tightened at the vivid memory, causing Nicholas to nearly groan aloud as he shifted to relive the pressure at the front of his trousers. It was pure torture to sit here and stare at her, but Nicholas found he couldn't bring himself to move back to his own seat.

While the phrase "look but don't touch" hammered across his brain, Nicholas found himself unable to comply. He leaned forward, wrapping one of her curly auburn strands of hair around his finger, feeling the soft texture slide across his fingertips. As he lifted his hand to her cheek, Isabelle nestled her face into his palm, her breath warm on his skin. She sighed, the sound creeping around the edges of his self-control. All he had to do was move closer, bringing her lips into closer proximity to his and press his mouth to hers. He could almost imagine how she would taste. No, he didn't dare allow his thoughts to drift, not again.

If only this were another time, another place, Nicholas would have lifted her in his arms and carried her off to the back of the plane, to his private bedroom, and made love to her. Under present circumstances that should be the last thing he considered, nor did he imagine Isabelle would be receptive to his advances.

Now, his fingers itched to tuck the wayward curl that fell across her cheek back behind her ear, but he didn't. He didn't want to disturb whatever sweet dreams she was currently having. More importantly, he didn't want to say or do anything to make her doubt her decision to go with him to Wellfleet Isle. Instead, Nicholas sat there for the next half hour and just observed Isabelle in slumber, his mind filled with memories of the past.

*

Isabelle felt him staring at her, even with her eyes closed. Goosebumps dotted her forearms at the realization he was close, close enough to touch should she reach out her hand toward him. For a moment, she forgot where she was and why the ground seemed to be vibrating beneath her feet. She opened her eyes, and then quickly sat up straighter in the chair, suddenly conscious of her surroundings.

The Corsair's private jet.

Nicholas.

On her way to Wellfleet Isle to care for the king.

The memories rushed back, causing her heartbeat to quicken. She caught sight of the man less than three feet from her, and the air left her lungs in a rush. In her quest to ignore the take-off of the plane, Isabelle allowed her thoughts to wander. She'd been having the nicest daydream of kissing Nicholas. Of him touching her, touching her face with his hand, of him coming closer, then closer still before… Heat rushed to her face.

Isabelle fought the urge to run her fingers through her hair and check her appearance in her compact. Doing so would alert Nicholas to the fact she felt nervous around him. And right now that was the last thing she wanted.

When Nicholas turned to look out the window, Isabelle allowed her gaze to sweep over him. He appeared so calm sitting there, suit coat now discarded. His tie loosened at the neck, the top button of his shirt open and the cuffs of his shirtsleeves rolled back exposing tanned, muscular arms sprinkled with dark, crisp hair. He tapped his fingers lightly on the seat. Looking that good ought to be illegal, she thought.

She gulped and retrained her eyes on the window and away from him. Bright blue water spread out below the plane and white, fluffy clouds rose above them for as far as the eye could see. Her stomach gave a lurch and Isabelle quickly shifted her gaze back to him, knowing full well it had nothing to do with the altitude and everything to do with the man seated next to her. Darn him for being able to affect her so deeply without even looking in her direction.

"We should be arriving on Wellfleet within the next two hours. Would you care for something to eat or drink?" He swung his gaze back to her and Isabelle quickly averted her eyes, so as not to be caught staring.

Her stomach growled loudly, betraying her need to say no. "That would be nice. Thank you."

With a flick of his wrist, within seconds a linen covered table set for two was wheeled between them. Lifting the cup of tea to her lips, Isabelle inhaled the enticing aroma, letting it seep into her senses before taking a sip. Amazingly enough, the tea contained just the right amount of lemon and honey as if she'd prepared it herself. Somehow the knowledge that Nicholas remembered how she drank it did nothing to settle her.

"I trust everything is to your satisfaction," Nicholas inquired.

"Somehow I believe you already know the answer, but yes, everything is wonderful," Isabelle replied, trying to keep the hint of sarcasm out of her voice as she took another sip of tea. And all the more so, everything tasted so good it made it hard to stay mad at him.

His only reaction to her semi-rude comment was to lift his eyebrow in her direction and smile at her.

Without saying a word, the man knew how to push her buttons and get a rise out of her. Whether he meant to or not was an entirely different story.

"I hoped you'd brought a dossier on the king so I could familiarize myself with his case before we arrive on Wellfleet Isle. What little I know about your father is from what I've read in the newspapers since yesterday, and I'm sure there's much more to the man than that."

"Regretfully, I did not bring any of my father's files with me on this trip. But I assure you everything you need will be accessible upon our arrival."

Somehow, regret seemed the furthest thing possible from the look on his face. Isabelle could wait until she arrived at the palace, but would have preferred the travel time on the plane to study up on the king and his medical history.

"Do you ever think about us?" Nicholas asked, effectively changing the subject to an entirely new and off-base topic.

Isabelle nearly choked on the sip of tea, the hot brew practically scalding her tongue as she reached for a napkin, her hands shaky. Clenching them into fists around the cloth, she hid them in her lap.

"I really don't see what that has to do with anything at the moment."

"Humor me. Call it for old time's sake, if you will."

Isabelle had the feeling Nicholas already knew the answer to his question. "I did for a while, but when you never came back, I—"

"You what?" Nicholas leaned forward, interest lighting his face as he rested his elbows on the table, awaiting her response.

What was she supposed to say? Of course she thought about the two of them. For the longest time it was all she'd thought of and nothing else. After a while, it became easier to push the memories back, bury them, and look toward building a new future.

"When you didn't come back, I moved on with my life. The same as you. After a while you don't miss what you never really had." She shrugged. "I'm here to do a job, not relive past indiscretions. And as such, I think it only fair to let you know this arrangement is strictly professional, with my caring for your father, the king. There's nothing between us anymore. I'll work with you and for you, but that's where it ends." Isabelle folded her hands in her lap, squeezing her fingers so tightly she could see the white tinge to her knuckles.

"I see. As you wish."

The jab hit home as Isabelle watched his posture became ramrod straight, no emotion visible on his face, the tone of his voice distinctly more formal. Apparently that wasn't the answer he'd been expecting. And from his reply, Isabelle didn't know whether to laugh or cry. But it was the truth; she meant what she said. They were not a couple any more. There was no way she going to allow herself to be romantically involved with Nicholas Corsairs ever again.

*

Isabelle fumbled with the seatbelt, her fingers clumsy, her movements jerky. The harder she tugged, instead of releasing the clasp it seemed to tighten it. Darn the man for making her want him after all this time.

"Allow me to assist you." Nicholas stood and leaned across her.

"I've got it." The scent of his citrus aftershave wafted across her senses, causing Isabelle to momentarily lose her single-minded focus. The man was incorrigible. Had he heard nothing she said to him?

Their fingers meshed on the nylon strap, and she felt the familiar tug of electricity. She unconsciously licked her lips, and then looked up to find Nicholas's face mere inches from her own. Isabelle watched his pupils darken to an even deeper shade of blue as she continued to stare at him. Her nipples tightened to hard nubs beneath her blouse, and for a second her emotions teetered. How easy it would be to touch his lips one more time, feel the warmth of his mouth against hers.

No, no, no. This would never do, she mentally chastised herself. Here it was seconds later and she was already breaking her own rule of nothing more than business between the two of them. Isabelle gave the seatbelt a hard tug and the clasp released with a loud clang. Jumping to her feet, Isabelle tried to put distance between the two of them but came up short against the edge of the seat.

"I think I'll go freshen up before we land." Her excuse sounded lame even to her own ears, as she fled to the restroom at the rear of the plane. Except this wasn't anything like the restroom on any planes she'd ever been on. First she had to pass through a bedroom with a large bed centered within. The image of Nicholas in that bed popped into her head and Isabelle bit her lip. No, she didn't want to think about Nicholas in that bed, didn't want to think about him in anyone's bed or anyone sharing his bed. It gave new meaning to the phrase "mile high club" and Isabelle hurried into the bathroom and shut the door behind her to stop the naughty picture that lingered.

Locking the door behind her, Isabelle stared at her reflection in the vanity mirror. Her cheeks flushed, her breathing erratic, the last thing she needed to be thinking about was kissing Nicholas. Those days were gone.

She headed back toward her seat. Nicholas was now in his own chair across the aisle. As much as she tried to convince herself otherwise, a small part of her felt bereft from his closeness.

He stood as she drew near, waiting for her to sit before he did.

"Would you like anything else before we begin our descent into Wellfleet Isle?"

Isabelle shook her head. "No thank you. I'm fine."

He dropped a nod in her direction and waved off the flight attendant. Isabelle wondered if everyone always stood in anticipation of Nicholas's needs.

She heard the high-pitched whine as the wheels of the plane lowered and her panic began anew. Her hands shook as she quickly refastened the seatbelt for landing.

"Isabelle, look at me." His voice was low and commanding.

She turned her head, caught his stare head-on, and gulped as the plane bounced a bit from turbulence.

"Focus on my face. Don't look away, keep looking at me. In a few minutes we're going to land at the private airfield my family owns. We'll be on the ground and off the plane within minutes. Once you're on the tarmac, you'll be able to see the ocean from the runway. The bright blue waters of the Caribbean surround the palace on three sides. In my opinion, there is nothing like it in the world. You'll smell the tang of the salty air, taste it on your tongue, and feel the trade winds as they whisper over your skin, calling to you with their siren song."

She nodded, mesmerized by his words, the rich timbre of his voice lulling her into a state of tranquility, drawn in by the vivid images he verbally painted. "It sounds lovely. Tell me about the palace where you live." Tell me anything, Isabelle thought, just keep talking to me so I can forget about the plane landing.

"The palace is made of sandstone. A pale coral shade carved from over a hundred craftsmen many years ago. My grandparents were the first to live there, then my parents, and now I have the pleasure. The stained glass mosaics in the upper bedroom windows were brought over from Italy as a present to my great-grandmother from her parents as a wedding gift."

"It sounds absolutely gorgeous." Her nervous stomach slowly settled as Isabelle listened to Nicholas talk. For that matter, he could have talked about the weather as long as he kept her mind occupied until they touched the ground.

"You will be pleased to know each bedroom overlooks the ocean, so the sound of the waves will be your night music. There is nothing like being lulled to sleep by the sea. The palace has over seventy-five rooms and is the equivalent of the Windsor Castle in size. We generate our own electricity with wind power, utilize the sun for solar energy, and have a sustainable garden for produce year round. The rocky shore that lines the two sides of the palace provides us with protection from the elements. The third side is a white sugar sand beach we use as a private beach for family and personal guests. I welcome the opportunity to show you around my home and my country. It will give the people a chance to see you, meet you, and talk to you."

"I'd like that very much."

"As would I," Nicholas replied. "But first, shall we disembark?" A sexy grin crossed his features as he popped his seatbelt, stood and held out a hand to Isabelle.

She frowned, and then looked out the window. They had landed at the Wellfleet Isle airstrip and workmen were already unloading the baggage from the plane.

"We're already on the ground." Surprised, Isabelle released her seatbelt, stood and reached for her coat and purse.

"Is that all right?" He seemed confused by her statement.

Isabelle nodded. "Yes, I didn't realize we landed. I never felt the plane touch the ground."

Nicholas smiled. "That's because you were enjoying my description of the palace so much I didn't feel the need to immediately inform you that we had touched down."

As she walked toward the exit, Isabelle paused briefly, then turned to face Nicholas and placed her hand on his arm. A jolt of electricity raced up her arm at the brief contact. "Thank you."

"For what reason, may I ask?"

"For keeping my mind occupied while we were landing. You know how much take-off and landing scares me. I appreciate your kindness."

Nicholas lifted her hand to his lips and placed a soft kiss on her skin. His warm breath fanned the back of her hand, his lips lingering over the spot. "Kindness had nothing to do it with it, my dear Isabelle. It was my pleasure."

Damn the man. She could have stamped her foot in frustration. Isabelle didn't want to remember the way he made her feel. In fact, she'd tried everything possible to forget. Her eyes widened as she recalled one very vivid memory from the past of his eyes one minute filled with sleep, then the next ablaze with desire as he rolled her beneath him in their double bed. She could almost feel the touch of his hands stroking her body to a fevered pitch. Her need for him so great, she'd been willing to do almost anything for his touch.

But not anymore. No longer was she a lovesick girl, dreaming of white weddings, newborn babies, and picket fences. Those days were gone, struck down by the cruel reality of life.

She fought the urge to pull her hand away and tuck it behind her back. Instead, Isabelle smiled and tried to make light of the moment. The man made her think things she didn't want to think, but worse yet, he was beginning to make her realize how much she'd given up in her life. All of this within the past twenty-four hours.

*

Isabelle leaned back in her chair on the marble patio of the royal palace. The warm, tropical breeze fanned her skin as she lifted her face to the sun. Bringing the glass of ice tea to her lips, she took a sip before speaking.

"Your earlier description of Wellfleet Isle pales in comparison to the real thing. I see why you're so proud of your country. It's beautiful here. I'd never want to leave." Lush, thick greenery, brightly colored tropical flowers, and the sound of the waves crashing on the shore teased her senses into overload. What little Nicholas told her on the flight about his home didn't do the island justice. The things he'd left out were even more enchanting.

"Being surrounded by water gives us the advantage of the trade winds. The beaches on the island are white sugar sand, the water is always a consistent 74 degrees, even in December, and the weather is sunny for the most part. The island gets an average of 330 days of sunshine per year. Funny when I was younger, I couldn't wait to grow up and leave all this behind. Now I can't imagine any place else I'd rather be."

His words caught her unaware as Isabelle fought down the wave of nostalgia they carried with them. She tried to focus her thoughts on anything else rather than allow the past to rear its ugly head.

"Tell me about the hospital. When was it built? How many people can you accommodate during an emergency or otherwise?"

Nicholas shifted in his seat at the wrought iron table, bringing his knees in contact with hers. The simple act sent tremors across her skin. How could she still be so attracted to him? Time dulled the physical pain, but hadn't eased the passion.

Thankfully unaware of her reaction, Nicholas replied to her questions. "The hospital was built in nineteen eighty-five, but has since undergone numerous renovations. We have a full staff and the equipment necessary so residents don't have to fly to the mainland for their medical care. We are well suited to handle the majority of surgeries and a helicopter is on standby round the clock for anyone who requires immediate transport or evacuation."

"Sounds as though you've covered all the bases to make the hospital stand alone and be self-sufficient."

"Not yet, there are still things to be put into place, but I hope to have that all settled within the next couple of years. More plans are in the works."

"What you've accomplished so far is incredible."

"Thank you." Nicholas dipped his head slightly in response to her words.

He continued to stare at her before sliding a large manila file across the table. "This is my father's complete medical history. Before you meet him, I ask that you read the contents."

Isabelle felt the intensity of his gaze sweep her from head to toe, and she felt a flush work its way upward from her stomach. She lifted an eyebrow quizzically. "Is there a particular reason why you would prefer I read it ahead of time? Normally, I tend to meet the patient first, see how they describe what's going on, hear the symptoms they present with, and then assess for myself how I proceed. Then I'll read the previous medical documentation if there is any. And I'll want to discuss the options with the thoracic surgeon and the team at Wellfleet Hospital. Unless you have a problem with that, Nicholas?"

"Not at all. I defer to your judgment, Doctor Tandori." Nicholas leaned back in his chair and toyed with the droplets of condensation on the glass, rubbing his finger back and forth across the moisture.

The simple action robbed Isabelle of her ability to breathe. She couldn't pull her gaze away from his long, bronzed fingers caressing the glass. Wrenching herself from her clearly delusional thoughts, Isabelle pressed forward. "Another thing, if I'm to care for your father, then you must understand I have the final say in how the king will be cared for. No second guessing my decisions, micro-managing my orders, having your staff report back to you what I say or do, or I guarantee you'll find me on the next plane out, with or without your permission."

Isabelle waited for him to disagree, but he didn't. Instead, he suppressed a smile before answering. "Agreed. But I ask that you keep me informed of your decisions in regard to my Father's care and treatment, whether or not I agree with your findings."

She nodded. "I have no problem with that whatsoever. I'll be happy to give you regular updates in regard to my treatment plan."

He grinned at her, and then raised his glass in a mock salute. "Shall we eat? I know Cook will be dismayed if her lobster salad goes untouched. After lunch, I'll show you around the grounds if you're not too tired from your travels."

She hoped to at least visit with the king after lunch. "Thank you, but I don't want to keep you from your duties. There must be things you need to attend to, since you were away from the palace."

"Right now, my duty is to ensure you have everything you need to properly care for my father."

And right now every inch of Isabelle's body was screaming for her to stay as far away from Nicholas as possible. But present circumstances would force her to do the opposite. The situation warranted she work with him, not against him, regarding his father's care. If by doing so gave her the strength needed to get through the days and nights ahead, and keep Nicholas out of her thoughts, that's what Isabelle would do.

Never again would she allow herself to be dependent on a man as in the past. Waiting for someone to take care of her, instead of putting her needs first. Waiting for someone who never thought to tell her he was leaving, nor contact her at any time during the past ten years. And waiting for the sound of his footsteps on the stair steps that never came. Isabelle learned the hard way what it meant to be on her own and she'd done everything in her power never to be put in a position to let a man run her life. By doing so she'd created a nice, comfortable existence with a condo she'd furnished with all the comforts one could want, a job she loved at a hospital that was first choice on her list, and she wasn't about to look back and dwell on her regrets.

Nicholas's leaving had been like a knife, driven in deep and twisted hard. His unexpected departure, followed by the loss of their unborn baby, almost too much to bear. But she'd pulled herself together and faced down each day until graduation, after that throwing herself into her work with a vengeance. Later, getting her career established had eaten up the empty hours of the day until she no longer noticed.

She watched Nicholas wipe his mouth with the cloth napkin, then motion for the table to be cleared.

"If you have no objection, I have a few phone calls to return, and then I'm free to show you around the palace."

She made to protest, but he stopped her with an upraised hand. "I assure you, my time is my own. To do with what I want, when

I want, and I would very much like the honor of showing you my home and country."

Rather than make a scene, Isabelle merely nodded and acquiesced. "As you wish, your highness."

"You don't have to address me as such, at least not in private." His sexy smile outshone the sun and Isabelle's heart skipped a beat. Darn the man for being so good looking.

"Keep it up and I'll tell you exactly what you can do with that title of yours," she responded, her own smile hard to contain.

"Another challenge, Doctor Tandori? I'm intrigued by your suggestion. Though I might have a few of my own to offer in return." Nicholas pushed back his chair and stood. "Now, if you'll excuse me, I'm off to tend to business. We'll meet back here at three o'clock?"

Nicholas bent down and pressed his lips to her cheek. She couldn't think, couldn't breathe, and couldn't do anything with him this close. Her mouth refused to form words, so all she did was nod. For once in her life, Isabelle Tandori was speechless. Her gaze lingered on the man who strode off down the hall. Without conscious thought, Isabelle lifted her fingers to her face, tenderly touching the spot. She was in big trouble already.

Chapter Four

If he hadn't walked away from Isabelle when he did, Nicholas was sure she'd have seen the look of surprise that crossed his face. The feel of her skin beneath his lips, the quick intake of her breath all made him think things he shouldn't.

"I would be quite interested to know if you share Denton's assessment in regard to the doctor's appearance. Appease an old man, would you, my son?"

Nicholas reigned in his errant thoughts at his father's words. His father's previous physician, Doctor Algiers, a very capable health care professional, was older, stout, and bald.

"Father, as I previously stated, Doctor Tandori's medical background is quite extensive and her qualifications are stellar by comparison to other physicians of her caliber. That is why I have hired her, not because of her looks."

He wasn't about to tell his father anything about Isabelle's physical attributes. As it was, Nicholas had a hard enough time keeping his eyes off her generous curves, the poise with which she carried herself and the way she tucked her hair behind her ear that only emphasized the slender lines of her very kissable neck. She had definitely matured since their time together.

"Yes, yes I know. New times warrant new medicine, new doctors, and new treatments. Though I wonder if these newfangled signs of the time are really worth it. When a body is as old and tired as mine, what can you really do other than allow it to rest?"

The reality of his father's illness never failed to bring Nicholas to his knees, causing him to question every decision made in regard to the king's medical care. Before his own emotions got out of check, Nicholas pushed to his feet. "Father, you are not that old."

"My heart is failing, whether you want to believe it or not, I have accepted the ultimate outcome. No one can live forever and no one should want to either. We take what is offered us on this earth and live life to the fullest. No one can predict their own future, though many have tried. What will be is what will be in the end. You cannot change the course of time."

The king patted Nicholas on the cheek and Nicholas wondered who was comforting whom at that moment. This was not what he wanted to hear, especially now. It was as though his father had given up and that was simply not acceptable to Nicholas. A member of the royal family did not willingly give up, nor give in. The king had closed his eyes and seemed to be once more asleep. With a sigh, Nicholas leaned over the bed, pressed a kiss to his father's forehead, and turned toward the door.

"Sleep well, Father."

*

Nicholas paced back and forth in his private living quarters thinking about his father. He would do anything; move heaven and earth to keep the man alive and well. If only he could have done the same for his mother. By the time Nicholas had been summoned, his mother was dead. Clenching his fists in frustration, he fought the urge to slam his hand against the sandstone wall, knowing full well to do so would accomplish nothing but break bones in the process.

If only he had been notified sooner, he might have been able to make a difference. He would have...

What would he have done? The same as ten years prior. Drop everything and rush back to his mother's side, assuming his responsibilities as heir to the throne while his father prepared for a royal funeral. Nicholas refused to give in to his grief for fear of being construed as weak. He needed to stay strong for his father and brother. He needed to stay strong for the people of his country. He needed to stay strong because if he gave in to the agony, he might never return from it. If only Isabelle had been by his side, easing his pain and sorrow as only she could. But duty called and Nicholas obeyed, leaving her behind.

He felt guilty enough not being able to return to the palace in time to see his mother before she took her final breath, arriving thirty minutes too late. Reliving the past would not give him comfort, instead would open up a wealth of questions for which Nicholas had no answers. The first being why he waited so long to contact Isabelle.

How was he to make Isabelle understand that duty came first, in this case family, as it should? He would have liked to share this pain with the one person who meant the most to him in the world, someone who might understand and help him bear the brunt of it. Isabelle had been crystal clear in how estranged she was from her parents, how she basically raised herself because they didn't care to raise a child, and how by doing so made her a stronger, more determined person. Even back then, Isabelle had no qualms that being dependent on them would be her downfall. So she'd kept her distance on purpose, kept their hurtful and insensitive comments at bay by never taking them to heart. The idea was so foreign to Nicholas, that to this day he couldn't fathom a life without his father or brother in it.

How could he explain that caring for his father, for Aidan and for a country in turmoil due to the loss of a beloved matriarch took every second of every day? That in time, the days blended into one another as time crept past and his priorities changed, his life no longer his own.

Damn it all, what Nicholas wanted always seemed to fade to the background. By being a prince, he would never be able to give Isabelle what she wanted. A normal life with a normal man by her side.

*

Isabelle stared in awe at the suite of rooms she'd been given for her stay. The living room alone was the size of her entire condo in Chicago. But it was the bathroom that snagged her attention. A large soaking tub set at the far end of the room with fixtures that looked as though carved from stone, facing a wall of windows that looked out at the ocean. The bright blue waters of the Caribbean seemed to extend from the edge of the window clear to eternity. Isabelle knew once she climbed into the tub, she'd have a hard time wanting to leave. Her breath hitched as her imagination ran wild. Nicholas in the tub, watching as Isabelle climbed in, settling herself against his body. Cradled between his powerful thighs, her head resting on his shoulder as he washed every inch of her skin, dipping into the crevice between her thighs.

Isabelle started, her breath harsh in the quiet of the room. She needed to rein in her thoughts immediately, away from the sensual road trip her mind was taking. Every step of her life was planned, calculated to the nth degree toward a satisfactory result. But this…this was like throwing caution to the wind with her runaway thoughts.

Pushing the balcony doors open, she wandered outside. The sound of the waves reached her ears. The thought of sinking her toes into the warm, white sand as the waves lapped at her ankles brought back memories of a quick winter trip to Florida she and Nicholas had taken on spring break in college.

But more than that, she remembered it was the first time Nicholas told her he loved her as they sat side-by-side in the sand. The pain the memory brought with it caused her to feel the bite of her nails into the tender skin of her palms. Her knees shook so hard it was as though she'd just run a marathon.

"I will not allow the memories to overshadow what happened. Never again," she told herself aloud.

Isabelle turned and walked back through the suite. She sat down on the sofa and let her body melt into the fluffy cushions. Closing her eyes, she gave herself a moment to relax.

Isabelle found herself thinking how easily she could get used to this at the end of a hard day. With a rueful shake of her head, she opened her eyes. This was the last thing she should be getting used to. Being here was only temporary and she needed to remember that. Isabelle had a job to do, and then she would go back to the States and resume her own life. If it weren't for His Highness Nicholas Corsairs and his outlandish royal decision she come to Wellfleet, she'd be doing that right now.

Isabelle stood beside Nicholas as he pointed out the various rooms on each level. Her head swam from all the information.

"This is the administrative wing. Anything you require, please ask either Adele or Mary. Adele works for the palace as a whole, and Mary is my personal secretary. They have explicit instructions to assist you with whatever you need."

Nicholas cupped her elbow and led her across the hall to another set of double doors. The gentle pressure of his fingers on her skin sent a shiver down Isabelle's spine. Just being near him was doing crazy things to her insides. Two men jumped to attention when Nicholas entered the room.

"Please return to your duties." He dismissed the men then turned to Isabelle, continuing their tour. "This is the security office. Twenty-four hours a day guards are posted around the perimeter of the property and within the palace walls."

Isabelle noticed the guards earlier and caught a glimpse of one in the hallway only a few minutes prior.

"Did you have bodyguards when you were in Chicago?"

"But of course, they are full-time. They protect the royal family." He seemed confused by her question.

"Is there really a need for round-the-clock security in Wellfleet?"

Nicholas looked at her oddly. "There is always a need for

caution, no matter where you are. It is better to be prepared than caught unaware."

An apt way of putting it, Isabelle thought. Exactly the way she felt ten years prior when she'd come home to find him packing. She needed to put the past out of her mind and focus on the job at hand. Otherwise, she'd go insane before her six months were up.

"Ah, the car has arrived. If you aren't bored to tears already, I suggest a drive through the village." He looked at his watch then continued. "It's too late today for a tour of the medical facility, but I will make arrangements for you to view Wellfleet Hospital at your earliest convenience."

"No, I wasn't bored at all." If anything she was even more confused by the man standing by her side than before. She saw a totally different person than the one she knew from college and right now wasn't so sure what to make of him. "A drive into town would be wonderful. Thank you for suggesting it."

*

"So, dare I ask what you think of Wellfleet?" Nicholas asked as they strolled down the main street of town, a security guard trailing behind at a discreet distance.

"It's an amazing place, from what I've seen of it." Isabelle couldn't get over the colors of the buildings. The pale pastels seemed to blend in with the surroundings as though they'd been there forever, seeming to have sprung from the rocks themselves. The outside of the hospital was clean, well-tended to, and very modern by all standards. The village itself was quaint with lots of character. The people were warm and friendly, though she was a stranger. But being with Nicholas chased away all their doubts. They'd expressed well wishes for the king, for which Nicholas thanked each person by name, telling them he would let his father know they inquired after him.

"Here doctor lady, these are for you."

A small boy ran up to Isabelle and presented her with a handful of pink daisies.

Surprised by the touching gesture, Isabelle accepted the flowers from his outstretched hands. "Thank you, they're beautiful."

The boy smiled shyly and ran back to his mother, who hugged him tightly.

"The people are very caring. Some have lived on the island since before I was born. Anything that will help my father and the royal family will help the people."

Isabelle considered his words carefully without commenting. Right now she felt it best to observe rather than speak.

Watching him interact with the people in town opened her eyes to a whole new side of Nicholas. He was a man completely confident in his own skin, sure of his place in life, and secure enough to easily handle any situation that arose. An older woman ran out from the crowd gathered in front of the bakery, dropped to her knees and wept openly at Nicholas's feet for his ailing father.

One of his guards stepped forward ready to intervene, but Nicholas motioned him away with a flick of his wrist and a quick shake of his head. As Isabelle watched, Nicholas helped the woman to stand, handed her his handkerchief to dry her tears, and patted her hand all the while thanking her for her concern. He acted as though she wasn't an inconvenience, but someone who was genuinely concerned about his family. Too many times in the past Isabelle had seen doctors and even laypeople act as though their time was more precious than someone else's. To Nicholas, this woman was as valued a person as he was.

All the while, Isabelle couldn't fight the niggling recollection of the way they'd parted ten years prior. How come he hadn't shown her the same consideration he did for the woman only a minute ago? Why hadn't he listened to her concerns as he raced out the door? Yet, none of that mattered anymore. What mattered was the job she was hired to do.

Isabelle wandered down the streets of the town, her gaze caught on the shop windows. One in particular. The delicate, lacy nightgown drew her attention immediately, the intricate pattern of the lace obviously handmade.

"It is absolutely gorgeous."

"Yes it is. A man would be extremely lucky to have his woman waiting for him wearing that."

She felt the flush racing up her cheeks at his words.

"Though I myself find it more enticing to be the one removing the garment, one inch at a time, delaying the inevitable as it slips down over my lady's arms, pooling at her waist, then allowing the gown to drop to the floor forgotten as we move on to more pleasurable pursuits."

Isabelle shivered at the thought of being that woman. She forced herself not to look at him, instead focusing on his reflection in the storefront window.

"Would you like to go in and purchase it? I don't mind waiting."

She quickly shook her head. "Oh no, I couldn't."

"As you wish," was Nicholas's only response.

And wish she could. Just the thought of his words had her body strung tight, her nerves on high alert, and her mind thinking things she shouldn't. All the while Nicholas maintained a proper distance from Isabelle, never touching her, and never had mere words sounded more erotic to her ears.

She took a step to her right, not realizing the curb dropped off. Isabelle tried to catch herself before she fell, but felt nothing but air. Then suddenly she was brought up tight against a warm, solid wall of muscle and flesh.

"Are you all right?"

Isabelle inhaled the scent of his cologne, a combination of Nicholas and citrus rolled into one, wafting through her senses.

"I'm fine. I didn't see the curb, I guess." Isabelle knew she should step away, back up, anything, but couldn't get her feet to cooperate.

Against her forehead, Isabelle felt the five o'clock stubble on Nicholas's cheek. It was all she could not to shift her head, to feel the press of his whiskers to her skin, but didn't dare. Luckily, Nicholas spared her the effort as he set her from him, his hands still holding her elbows, his gaze skimming over her body, assessing her for injury. He waved away the shopkeeper that came out from the store.

"Are you certain you didn't injure yourself? I'd be very happy to examine you more thoroughly somewhere private." A devious grin crossed his mouth.

Isabelle gulped. The man was absolutely incorrigible. As enticing as the idea sounded, it was very dangerous to get carried away with such ideas. She shook her head. "I'm fine, really."

"Well then, if you are sure, shall we dine here tonight?"

Nicholas turned her toward the steps of the outdoor café, his hand warm on the curve of her spine.

Isabelle pulled her gaze away from the people on the sidewalks and looked toward the richly painted building with the colorful awning. "Of course, if you'd like," she murmured, hoping to see more of the town before their tour ended. Though she knew there would be other days, other times when she could come explore Wellfleet Isle on her own.

As they entered, the proprietor rushed over, a tall thin man with gray hair who repeatedly bowed and welcomed Nicholas to his humble eatery. He spoke so quickly his words tumbled over themselves, leaving him tongue-tied and a tad embarrassed.

"Your highness, it is a great honor to have you here. Please I have a table all ready for you."

Nicholas clasped the man's hand in a warm welcome, and then motioned Isabelle to precede him to their table.

"Gustav, this is Doctor Isabelle Tandori. She will be caring for King Philippe. Gustav is the proprietor here."

He held her chair as Isabelle looked around the restaurant. They were the only ones in attendance that evening. She noticed the bodyguards at the door, their stoic figures barring the way for any more diners.

"Thank you for dining at my humble establishment."

Isabelle glanced at the door. "Are we the only patrons this evening?"

"Yes, I have closed the restaurant for your dining pleasure. It is a great honor Prince Nicholas bestows on my family. My restaurant thrives because he comes here. The tourists come to see where royalty dines, eat where the prince eats, and drink where the prince drinks." Gustav hurried off and returned momentarily with a bottle of wine and platter of bruschetta.

Nicholas shook off the man's praise with a lift of his hand. "Gustav exaggerates greatly. He has the best Italian food on the island. You will see for yourself why I come here to dine."

Isabelle stared at Nicholas. Was it really the only reason? From Gustav's over-the-top praise of Prince Nicholas, she wondered if there wasn't more to the man seated across the table from her.

A flurry of activity followed as the man brought his wife and two daughters out from the kitchen to see Nicholas. Again he spoke to everyone, shook their hands and then turned to introduce her to the family.

Isabelle saw the man blush at Nicholas's words of praise. Another round of bowing accompanied the well wishes of the family to Isabelle for her duty to the king. She wanted to tell them it wasn't as big a deal as they were making it out to be, but figured it best to leave things unsaid for the time being. This was a job, yet the Morales family acted as though it were a lifetime commitment of service to the Corsairs.

Lifting the piece of still warm bread to her mouth, Isabelle nearly groaned aloud as the fusion of flavors hit her tongue. The garlic, rosemary, and olive oil blended together to create something she'd never found in the States.

"This is delicious." She lifted her head to find Nicholas staring at her, a strange expression on his face, his jaw as though set in stone. "What?"

He shook his head. "You have a drop of olive oil on your chin. Allow me."

Nicholas reached across the table and slowly ran his thumb across Isabelle's chin, effectively capturing the spill. Leaning back in his chair, he casually swirled his tongue over the tip of his finger, removing all traces of the oil, his gaze locked on her face. A flash of something primitive lingered in his eyes. The action so erotic Isabelle felt the tug of arousal from the tip of her toes to the top of her head. The restaurant faded into the background as she stared at him, drawn in by the hypnotic lull of his eyes. It was all Isabelle could do not to purposely smear the dipping oil onto her face for a repeat performance.

"I wholeheartedly agree; it is delicious."

For some reason, Isabelle didn't think he was talking about the olive oil. Her thoughts scattered, she focused on picking up her wine glass and taking a sip, forcing her hand not to tremble.

"Doesn't it get to be old?" Isabelle asked when she got her racing heartbeat under control. She needed to steer the conversation in a different direction in order to maintain her sanity.

"I beg your pardon?" Nicholas shifted his gaze to her.

"Being called 'your highness' all the time. I would think it incredibly difficult to be so proper and formal all the time, never allowing the real you to show though. It would make things less complicated if you could just be yourself."

He was so different from the Nicholas she remembered. The Nicholas from ten years before, who laughed and joked all the time, smiling, happy, and relaxed. Such a huge contrast from the stiff and stilted man now seated across the table from her.

He actually had the audacity to look shocked at her question. "That is not possible."

"I don't see why not." Isabelle pressed her point forward.

Nicholas dropped his napkin on the table, a frown now marring the smooth tanned surface of his forehead as he apparently worked over her question in his head. "It just isn't done that way, Isabelle. I am not their best friend, nor their confidante. I am their leader. I decide what is right for my people, my country. And as such my being their 'pal' would hamper my ability to maintain the level of power needed to do my job."

The weight of the world was on his shoulders. It must be an awful way to live, Isabelle thought. Thankfully she didn't have to live this way. There was something in his tone that made her think she was missing something. Some small piece of the puzzle he refused to share about the afternoon he left town. It didn't make sense. He'd always been such a strong man, yet if he'd only let her in, maybe she could help.

"So basically when someone of the royal family says jump, the people have no option but to say how high?" Her ire up, Isabelle pushed further.

"That is not what I said. I would not expect you to understand the way things are done here on Wellfleet." Nicholas suddenly sounded defensive.

"And I suppose the same holds true for a member of the royal family? When you're summoned, you must obey?"

"Of course."

"The day you left, ten years ago. I walked in the door and you walked out. You never said a word to me about why you had to leave. You never told me you weren't who you said you were. Three years together and it was all a lie. I don't understand why you couldn't have said something, given me a reason for your leaving, or even called later to explain." Her voice cracked and Isabelle hated the way she sounded so needy. For the past twenty-four hours, she'd wanted to bring up their past, search for and get the answers she needed. And now that the time had come, Isabelle was scared to hear what Nicholas would say.

"I'm sorry Isabelle. You wouldn't understand. You couldn't." Nicholas avoided meeting her eyes.

Her body snapped to attention at his words for she had obviously hit a nerve. Try me, Isabelle wanted to say, but didn't. Something flitted across his face but was gone before Isabelle could make out what it was.

"I don't understand when you won't talk to me about it. I would've had the decency to at least tell you where I was going, instead of walking away and never looking back until now. Do you know what it feels like to have someone you care for walk out of your life and never give a reason? To wait for them to come back until every bone is your body is mentally and physically exhausted? No, of course you don't. No one in their right mind would do that to a member of the royal family. Not without fear of retribution."

"I do not wish to fight with you. This discussion is concluded." Nicholas shoved his hand through his hair and motioned for one of his bodyguards.

The man was truly insufferable. She wanted to scream at him, rally and tell him how much she needed him then, but Isabelle was stronger than that. She'd learned through the years to decide for herself the next best course of action.

"I am not one of your people, your subjects. I am here of my own free will." Sort of, Isabelle reminded herself, her anger now racing across every nerve ending in her body. "And as such, you best remember that. You are not *my* ruler."

*

"Thank you for the tour of your home, the town, and dinner too. If you'll excuse me, I've a lot of reading to do before turning in tonight. I want to be prepared when I see the king tomorrow." Isabelle started off down the hall, almost eager in her haste to get away from him. The last she wanted or needed was another argument with Nicholas. Their last one still rang in her ears.

"Allow me to escort you to your suite." He seemed distracted as they entered the palace, but placed his hand on the small of her back and turned her toward the doors to the private wing.

"You don't have to. I can find my way." Isabelle protested, though it was no use.

By way of a reply, Nicholas merely lifted his eyebrow.

She felt the heat of his hand through the cotton fabric of her top. The gentle pressure of his palm against her back teased at her. The sound of their footsteps echoed in the cavernous hallway. But it was the rapid fire beating of her heart that threatened to drown everything else. Despite their earlier argument, Isabelle felt sorry for Nicholas. She wondered if he knew how much faith the people put in him.

"If you should have any questions, please do not hesitate to call. The phone in your suite has a direct line to my room should you need me."

Her gaze widened as the last thing she wanted was to need Nicholas. She would not call his room in the middle of the night, or any other time. That was not going to happen. However he'd done it, within seconds they were at the door of Isabelle's suite.

"Thank you, but I'll manage. If I have questions in regard to your father's file, I'll ask Denton."

"As you wish. I would of course prefer that you speak to me as opposed to Denton. But the choice is yours. I defer to your decision. Goodnight, Isabelle." Nicholas turned from her door.

"Nicholas."

At the sound of her voice, his steps halted, his gaze lifting to her face.

She spoke reluctantly, not wanting to say it, but knowing she should. "I'm sorry if I overstepped my bounds tonight. I had no right to tell you how to run your country." Despite all of her earlier protestations, Isabelle knew it was the right thing to do. While she wouldn't apologize for the way she felt ten years ago, she would for tonight.

A small smile crossed his face, as some of the seriousness left his features. "I enjoy our verbal sparring and it appears you are the only one with enough courage to take me on, freely state the things that are on your mind without fear of reprisal. I hope that will never change. Now I bid you sweet dreams, Isabelle."

Nicholas dipped his head in a slight bow and leaned forward at the same time Isabelle shifted and reached for the doorknob. The kiss that should have landed on her cheek caught her directly on the lips, causing her to suck in a quick gulp of air before his mouth covered hers. For a brief second, everything seemed frozen in place and she gave herself up to the feeling.

Isabelle felt his hot breath against her mouth, the press of his lips touching her own and bit down a groan. His hand snaked around her neck, cupping the back of her head, pulling her closer as Nicholas increased the intensity of the kiss. She should have pushed him away, but didn't. Instead her fingers splayed across the front of his shirt, tangling in his crisp chest hairs at his opened collar, tasted the red wine they'd drank at dinner, and felt the heat of his body sear her. Then as abruptly as it started, it was over. Nicholas took a step back, his features back into a neutral emotionless mask and the contact between them broken. It was all Isabelle could do not to immediately touch her fingers to her lips.

Instead, she quickly fumbled for the knob, retreating into her room and shutting the door without saying a word to Nicholas. Leaning back against the massive wooden portal, she tried to get her ragged breathing under control. This was not supposed to happen and yet Isabelle couldn't think of anything she wanted more than the man outside her door right that very moment.

Darn him for turning her insides to knots. And darn him even further for making her remember just how wonderful his lips felt against her skin. With a stomp of her foot on the marble tiles, Isabelle marched across the living room into the bedroom beyond and threw herself down on the bed.

With her face buried in the pillows, she smacked her fists into the soft, silky comforter covering the bed. But the futile attempt did nothing to console her spiraling emotions. Six months was going to feel like an eternity at this pace.

*

Nicholas stood dumbfounded as he stared at the closed door of Isabelle's suite. He wondered if he looked as shell-shocked as he felt. What the hell just happened? One minute he was saying goodnight, the next his lips were on hers and his fingers tangled in her hair. He'd meant to kiss her cheek, but instead found himself indulging in the sweet taste of her lips as they softened beneath his touch. A wash of memories flooded over him and his stomach clenched. He tried to forget it happened, but it wasn't that simple. They kissed and he enjoyed it. Just as Nicholas had known he would. And just as he hoped it would happen again. Especially if he had anything to say about the matter. A smile crossed his face, and then was quickly replaced by a frown.

It shouldn't have happened and Nicholas refused to apologize for how he felt. But it wasn't what the future ruler should be doing no matter the reason, kissing the king's private physician in the corridor. It was the same at the restaurant. He wanted to reach across the table and hold her hand, feed her bites of his dessert, taste the wine that lingered on her lips after the meal. As it was, he'd lost control by touching her as he did, letting his finger trail across her skin, wiping the oil from her face, then tasting it for himself. His public persona forced him to remain impassive to the constraints she inflicted on his body. When she closed her eyes and sighed aloud at the richness of the tiramisu as she slid the fork into her mouth, if it were any other time and place, he would have hauled her into his arms and kissed her senseless. The public be damned.

But he was Prince Nicholas Corsairs, heir to the throne of Wellfleet Isle. He needed to compartmentalize his feelings for Isabelle, put them away at the back of his mind. What he wanted didn't matter. For a brief second, Nicholas wondered if it was all worth it.

Fisting his hands at his side, Nicholas turned on his heel, strode down the hall, and headed across the walkway that separated the family suites from the guest suites. Once in his suite, he stripped off his clothes, dropped them on the bedroom floor and entered the walk-in shower in his master bathroom. He turned the cold-water faucet as far as it would go, positioning his body under the stinging spray, letting the icy water sluice over his body. The cold did nothing to calm his raging hormones. If anything, it made things worse. How that was possible, Nicholas wasn't sure. Goosebumps rose on his arms as he held himself perfectly still, waiting for his emotions to cool off as quickly as his skin.

Within seconds, he was shivering from the effect and quickly adjusted the temperature to a warmer setting in an effort to stop his teeth from chattering. Scrubbing his hands over his face as though he could somehow erase the memory of what occurred; Nicholas closed his eyes and leaned back against the shower wall.

The image of Isabelle in his shower immediately filled his head, as he imagined lathering her body with his hands, dipping into every crevice of her body, burned into his brain.

Nicholas turned off the shower, stepped from the glass enclosure, and briskly ran the towel over his skin. He walked into the bedroom and lay on his bed. He laced his fingers behind his head and stared at the ceiling in hopes of trying to forget it happened. But it wasn't meant to be. The memory of the soft gasp he heard escape Isabelle's lips was enough to send his lower anatomy straight to full attention. The feel of the expensive silk sheets against his fevered flesh sent his body into sensory overload. Shifting on the bed to ease his discomfort, the sheet slid to one side, caressing his skin like a lover's touch, causing his already fragile control to further slip a notch.

Mentally counting to one hundred, Nicholas willed himself to relax. It was a simple issue of mind over matter. The brain controlled the body, not the other way around. At least that was what he kept telling himself, despite his bodies opposite reaction.

The idea of her challenging him at dinner drew a smile to his lips, despite everything else. She was a mother lioness when angered. Never backing down from the fight, never running for cover and more importantly, never knowing when to stop pressing her advantage. It was all he could do not to lean across the table and kiss her soundly in order to stop her questions.

But he couldn't. It wasn't to be done. His position demanded a higher standard from him. Kissing was not the answer, though it was definitely more pleasurable than dueling with words. Isabelle didn't understand the way things were done here on Wellfleet Isle. She couldn't know how much of an impact the royal family had on their people. It was his life and his duty to make sure the people thrived and businesses grew. He couldn't give two weeks' notice and leave his position.

His jaw tightly clenched, Nicholas turned his gaze toward the open balcony doors and saw the stars twinkling high in the night sky. He tried to focus on the sound of the waves to soothe his restless body and calm his jagged nerves, but found he couldn't give in as easily as other nights. Most certainly not to the waves lapping at the beach outside his door, but yet quite willingly to Isabelle.

The idea caused his groin to tighten once more and Nicholas knew only one way to ultimately satisfy the ache that plagued him. A most pleasurable way at that, though at this exact second he was probably the only one thinking it.

Nicholas pulled the pillow out from behind his head and threw it across the bedroom in frustration. It hit the wall with a soft thud and dropped to the floor. So much for taking his tension out on an inanimate object. Sleep would be a long time coming this evening. If at all.

Chapter Five

Isabelle rubbed at her eyes, gritty from lack of sleep, then squared her shoulders. It was time to meet the king and, for the first time in forever, she was actually nervous at seeing a patient. Whether for the fact he was royalty or not, Isabelle wasn't sure. Her patients ran the gamut from celebrities to the common man, and she'd never experienced a bout of anticipatory jitters like the one she currently experienced.

"Ready or not, here I come." She lifted her hand and knocked on the door to the king's suite.

The door opened immediately and Isabelle introduced herself to a man who looked to be in his sixties with graying hair and a slight build, though as Isabelle knew appearances could be deceiving.

"Good morning, I'm Doctor Isabelle Tandori."

"Good morning. I am Denton, the king's personal aide. The king is awake and has been apprised of your arrival." He motioned for her to precede him into the room.

"I'll see to it that the king has whatever he needs for this morning."

"As you wish, Doctor Tandori. Should you require assistance at any time, Karl will alert me. I'll be in my quarters."

Isabelle looked in the direction Denton pointed to find a security guard positioned by the French doors. Karl dropped a nod in her direction, but said nothing, his countenance dark and foreboding as he stood his ground.

She looked from the guard to the man in the chair, and then did a double take. It was like looking at Nicholas twenty years in the future. Everything down to the furrowed brow was the same.

For a brief second, Isabelle marveled at how handsome both men were, yet years apart in age. Then she pulled herself together in order to do the job she was here to do.

"Good morning, I'm Doctor Isabelle Tandori." Isabelle stuck her hand out in front of her, and then paused. Should she offer to shake his hand? Or maybe she was supposed to bow. Or maybe it was something entirely different. She'd never thought of that before.

Before she could blink, Karl was across the room and standing between her and the king, his gun drawn.

"Karl, for heaven's sake, she's a doctor, not an assassin. Please, go have some coffee and take a break. I'll be fine." The king waved the guard to step away.

"I'm so sorry, I wasn't sure what I was supposed to do. Apparently that was the wrong option." Isabelle took a step back, embarrassed by her faux pas.

"Nonsense. Everyone around here thinks I'm at death's door should I as much as sneeze." The king stuck his hand out in front of him for Isabelle to shake. "Welcome to Wellfleet Isle, my dear. There's never a dull moment as you just saw." A hint of a smile graced the king's face and Isabelle allowed herself to relax.

Isabelle bit back a smile before stepping forward to accept his outstretched hand. "It's a pleasure to meet you, your highness."

After shaking the king's hand, she moved to the side of the chair and reached for the cuff on the portable blood pressure machine. Fastening it around his arm, Isabelle pressed the button on the monitor screen.

"My son tells me you are the best at what you do in the States." The king focused his sharp blue-eyed gaze on Isabelle and again she was struck by the similarities between father and son. Nothing like getting right to the point and ignoring the pleasantries, Isabelle thought.

"Your son gives me far too much credit." He also assumes a lot of things that aren't true, as well. It was all she could do not to say the words aloud, but thought better of it. Instead, Isabelle watched the gauge, and then made a notation on the chart. After spending the better part of the evening reviewing the King's complete medical history, she'd slept fitfully for the other three hours. But the problem was whom she'd been dreaming of during that time: Nicholas. The man occupied too much of her thoughts within the past few days.

"So tell me what your diagnosis is?"

Isabelle smiled and removed the black wrap from the king's arm. "With all due respect, your highness, I'd be remiss if I jumped blindly to a diagnosis within five minutes of assessing you. Unless you'd prefer I accept what your former physician wrote in his notes regarding your care and treatment. If that's the case, I suggest your son rehire him and I'll go back to the States and resume my practice."

For a second, Isabelle feared she might have spoken out of turn. Then again, she didn't consider Nicholas or the king to be her superior in any way and she wasn't about to start now.

King Philippe looked narrowly at Isabelle, his blue-eyed stare so much like Nicholas that she fought the urge to cower and apologize, even against her better judgment. But she didn't. She stood there waiting for whatever would be.

After a moment, he chuckled. "Point well taken, Doctor Tandori."

Isabelle lifted his wrist and felt for a pulse. Her own was jumping rapidly all over the place as she tried not to flush at the compliment.

"Thank you. However, I did read through your medical file last night."

The king snorted. "Not exactly what I would call a pleasurable evening. You should be out dancing or dining; doing whatever it is you young people like to do nowadays."

Isabelle smiled and patted his hand. "Your care and comfort is first and foremost on my mind before dining and dancing. Unless of course you'd like to be my partner for an evening? I believe my calendar is quite open at present."

"If I were forty years younger, my dear, I'd take you up on that wonderful offer. But my dancing days are over for this lifetime. Would you care for some coffee?"

"I'd love some, allow me to pour." Isabelle lifted a cup from the coffee service off the desk and handed him the cup.

"Thank you, my dear, or would you prefer I call you Doctor Tandori?"

"Isabelle, please." She poured a cup of the rich aromatic blend and took a sip before walking back and settling herself on the chair beside the bed.

"Then you must call me Philippe."

Isabelle started, nearly spilling the hot coffee across her lap. "I can't do that. It wouldn't be right. At least I don't think it would."

"I do not understand why you can't do this?" The older man looked confused by her remark.

"Because you're the king," she sputtered. Her hands still shaky, Isabelle sat the cup on the table for fear of spilling it further.

"And as such I command you to call me Philippe."

For a moment, Isabelle could only stare at him, and then she gathered her wits about her. "Command me? I can see where your son learned it from." Except the king had a different opinion when it came to informality between commoners and royals.

"Headstrong boy, always has been, always will be. So unlike his brother Aidan. He is four years younger than Nicholas and more like his mother. Outgoing, gregarious, very much 'the life of the party.' Have you met him yet?"

"No, I haven't had the pleasure." Considering she didn't know about Aidan or any of the royal family until a mere forty-eight hours ago.

"Possibly he will be coming home at some point while you are here at Wellfleet."

Isabelle listened as the Philippe spoke of his family, the sound of his heartbeat evening out on the monitor, becoming more consistent as he relaxed and remembered the past. She sat quietly as he wove a wonderful tale of love telling her of his wife, Queen Julia, and her subsequent death from cancer.

"I'm sure you know of all of this already," he finished, handing her his cup.

"No, I didn't. What little I know, I know only of Nicholas," she answered truthfully. He'd never told her about any of the other members of his family, his mother's illness or subsequent death, or even that he had a younger brother. In fact, he never told her anything about being a royal at all.

"Your highness…" Isabelle stopped at the frown that suddenly marred his features. "Philippe, today would be the perfect day to take lunch on the patio. It's time you got out and breathed in some fresh air."

King Philippe shook his head. "It's too much trouble to eat out there."

"I was presumptuous enough to ask that lunch be brought at eleven. The plans are already underway and we will be dining on the terrace, Philippe."

Philippe chanced a glance at the clock on the bedroom wall. "Is this something you learned in your medical books? To bully the patients into doing what you want them to do?"

For a moment Isabelle hesitated, then firmly stood her ground. "No, it's something that life has taught me. Giving up is not the answer, persevering ahead is. Now tell me, is this how you want your son to remember you?"

Isabelle knew she'd struck a nerve by the way his features changed. The dark countenance that came over his face was like an ominous thundercloud. The similarities between the King and Nicholas were glaring. They shared so many of the same mannerisms.

"What are you talking about, how my son would remember me." The king straightened his pajamas, and pushed his feet into his slippers.

Isabelle draped his robe over his shoulders as he made to stand and shuffled toward the balcony.

He looked at her and sighed. "Why does everyone make such a fuss over me? I'm an old man. My needs do not outweigh the needs of others."

"Your son loves you very much."

"Nicholas needs to focus his energies more on the people, the island, the future, and less on me."

She shook her head. "He can't when his thoughts are on helping you get well. He'll use whatever means necessary if it means you will live a long, healthy, happy life. Which you can do if you have the transplant surgery. The prognosis is excellent for a full recovery. But the decision must be yours. I cannot force you, though I can suggest and advise that you strongly consider it."

King Philippe started to speak, his voice low. "I loved my wife more than anything else on this earth. When she became ill, there was nothing I could do to save her. If only she'd come to me sooner, caught the illness early on, none of this would have happened. It could have been prevented but she chose to remain silent to her pain. I am the king and I could do nothing. The people were devastated, Nicholas and Aidan were devastated, and I was devastated."

Isabelle's heart ached for him. What a great love affair they shared. One she could only hope to have in her life. It was hard to speak past the lump firmly lodged in her throat. She reached out and took his hand in hers. "We can't go back and change the past. All we can do is focus on the present and the future in hopes of making things right."

He turned toward Isabelle and she saw the sheen of tears in his eyes.

"If only you were here, you might have been able to save her. Julia always spoke of wanting a daughter, but she loved her sons quite fiercely. She would have liked you very much, my dear Isabelle. Of that I am quite certain."

Isabelle couldn't speak for fear she'd cry. She nodded; words weren't necessary at that moment. The last thing she wanted was to let Philippe inside her heart, start liking him, and think of him as a friend rather than her patient during her stay. Isabelle needed to remind herself this was a job she'd been hired to perform. But in the short time she'd been in Philippe's room, he'd managed to get past the brick wall she'd built around her heart. Only one person had been able to do that and Isabelle didn't want to think of the consequences if the wall crumbled.

*

"Father, I never thought to find you out here."

Nicholas walked out onto the balcony, his heart in his throat. When he'd first entered the suite to find it empty, he'd been under the impression something terrible had happened. Then the sound of Isabelle's light and airy laughter caught his attention and drew him toward the open balcony doors. Yet the minute he walked onto the terrace, she stopped. What he wouldn't have given to linger a few minutes more in secret, if only to hear it again.

"Come join us, we're about to have dessert."

Nicholas looked at his father, then at Isabelle. "I am quite pleased to see you up and about."

"Sit, sit." His father motioned to the empty chair. "Isabelle and I enjoyed quite a pleasant lunch on the terrace. Though at first I wasn't sure, but your lovely Doctor Tandori here didn't give me much of a choice."

His lovely Doctor Tandori.

The words caused Nicholas's lower extremities to quicken. He turned his gaze to Isabelle and found her blushing, the sight quite appealing. She crossed her legs and Nicholas followed the movement. Bright pink painted toenails peeked out at him from under the hem of her pants, her sandals discarded nearby. The sight of those bare toes did something in the pit of his stomach that Nicholas couldn't explain and right now, he didn't want to try.

He draped his suit coat over the back of the chair. How he would have preferred to be here, with his father and Isabelle instead of cooped up in the hospital's conference room working out the terms of another building agreement. For the first time in a long time, Nicholas hadn't wanted to be at work.

"Well, I am thrilled to see you out here. I will join you for dessert."

"That is all due to Isabelle. She bullied me into eating out here."

"Now, Philippe, I did not bully. I merely suggested."

This was why he needed Isabelle here. Seeing how good she was for his father, getting the man to do things Nicholas had been unable to accomplish. A stab of guilt caught him between the ribs. Because of him, she was caring for his father, instead of doing what she loved back in the States. He forced her to come against her will, care for a man she knew nothing about, all to satisfy Nicholas.

Nicholas knew he couldn't take her away permanently from the life she'd built for herself. But until his father was back on his feet and the surgery over, Isabelle would remain on Wellfleet Isle. He'd lost his mother and Nicholas wasn't about to take a chance with his father's health. Isabelle never believed in changing her life for her family, but he did. There would no question of her leaving until that point. His mind was made up on the matter.

Isabelle passed the dessert plate to Nicholas. Their fingers collided and a spark of awareness shot up his arm from the brief contact. As Nicholas watched, she almost dropped the platter in her haste to get away from his touch.

It was good to know he wasn't the only one affected by their previous night's kiss. He'd tossed and turned long into the wee hours of the morning trying to escape the feel of her lips on his. The memory lingered, leaving him wanting more. Correct that: leaving him *needing* more. His dreams were interrupted with visions of her coming to him, kissing him, caressing him in his bed until Nicholas awoke frustrated and painfully aroused. Another cold shower had done nothing to quell the fire in his groin. At this rate, the palace would run out of cold water before Nicholas got his unruly hormones in check. "Philippe? She is calling you Philippe now?" Nicholas cocked an eyebrow in the direction of the king.

"Yes, is that a problem?" Philippe stared at his son oddly.

"Not at all. I just thought…" He didn't know what to think at present.

"Your father thought it easier to be more informal. I hope you don't mind." Her eyes dared him to challenge her as she flashed a triumphant grin his way.

Nicholas knew if they'd been alone she would have pushed his buttons as far as necessary in order to press her point home. She knew exactly where he stood on having commoners call him by his first name. Isabelle had always known how to get his ire up during their time together by calling him stuffy and arrogant. Two things he most certainly was not. Opinionated and decisive, quite possibly.

"Whatever you think best, father."

A muscle began to tic in his cheek. He couldn't keep his thoughts focused on the present, instead reliving their time together in the past. Waking up next to Isabelle, kissing her good morning, making love to her at night, and then repeating the process all over again the next day. He heard his father chuckle and Nicholas brought his wayward thoughts to the forefront.

"I trust you slept well last night, Doctor Tandori, being in unfamiliar surroundings?"

"Yes, I did. I fell asleep instantly thanks to the sound of the waves." Isabelle smiled at him, and then lowered her gaze back to her plate.

Nicholas tipped his head. She was lying as the smile that played about her mouth never quite reached her eyes. Over the years, he'd become an expert at reading body language. It was best to know right from the start who was a friend and who was foe before entering into the battle.

"So the hospital board was amenable to your suggestions regarding the new wing?" Philippe asked.

Nicholas wiped his mouth with the napkin before answering. "Yes, the maternity wing will open on schedule. There will be a ribbon cutting ceremony to officially commemorate the occasion."

Lately there were too many occasions when Nicholas felt stuck having to do something he didn't want to, but did anyway. Everything he'd done over the years had been with the idea that one day he'd go back to Maryland, back to practicing medicine, and back to Isabelle. Ten years later, he was still treading water in the same position at the deep end of the pool. Only Nicholas felt like he was drowning.

Isabelle made to stand. "Since the two of you need to discuss business, I'll excuse myself. Thank you, Philippe, for a very enjoyable day. Nicholas, enjoy the rest of your day."

"Good day, Isabelle."

Nicholas pushed his own chair back and stood. "Isabelle, I'll walk you out. Father, excuse me for a moment."

"Take your time, my son." The king lifted his water glass and Nicholas was pleased to see the steadiness of his father's hand.

Nicholas walked her to the door and paused, his hand on the knob, not allowing her to leave.

"I can't tell you how appreciative I am of your getting father out of bed and on the terrace. It has been a long time since I have seen him so talkative and happy, and I will forever be grateful to you."

Isabelle shook her head. "It was nothing really—"

He stopped her words with the gentle press of his fingers against her lips. "It was something, Isabelle. Please don't discount how much I am indebted to you. You already made a difference in my father's care. I look forward to hearing your assessment."

Nicholas moved his fingers from Isabelle's mouth before he opened the door and smiled at her. "Enjoy the rest of your day, Doctor Tandori. I know I shall, thanks to you."

His fingers tingled from the contact with her soft skin and warm breath. She looked back at him, moist lips parted, and it was all Nicholas could do not to pull her in his arms and show her just how grateful he was, but decided against it. For now at least.

*

Glancing down at the file in her hand, a part of her wondered once more why she'd been chosen to care for King Philippe. Any good cardiologist could take this case and do exactly what Nicholas was asking of her, as evidenced by the meticulous notes contained in the medical file.

For a brief second, Isabelle allowed herself the luxury of believing it was because of her shared past with Nicholas, then pushed away the notion. That left only her medical qualifications to explain why Isabelle was on Wellfleet Isle instead of back in Chicago braving the cold, wet elements of the spring weather.

She knew she should feel resentful at having been dragged away from her patients, resentful of the fact she'd no real say in the matter, and resentful her talents were being used on only one man, instead of many more whom could benefit from her education. She became a doctor to save people, lots of people, not just one man, albeit the King of Wellfleet Isle.

A niggling doubt wormed its way into her head. She didn't want to believe the only reason she was here was because of her past association with Nicholas, but could it be true? Everything moved along so quickly, his arrival in Chicago, how fast Isabelle needed to make a decision, how soon they'd gotten on the plane.

Isabelle tried to push the notion of him having feelings for her from her head. He didn't, did he? Yet from the minute their eyes met, he'd been the old Nicholas, the one she'd fallen in love with and couldn't wait to spend the rest of her life with. Of course, at times over the past few days he'd been Nicholas the prince, making decisions that only he could. A man who cared for his father, his country, and from what Isabelle could gather, about every person who lived here. But other times the sweet, kind, and loving man she remembered resurfaced and the lines blurred between old and new. Was she here because he still had feelings for her?

In her heart, Isabelle knew Nicholas wasn't a duplicitous man, and knew she was here for the right reasons. To help save a man's life: the King of Wellfleet Isle.

Right now Isabelle wanted to review the file in regard to the king. When she had all the facts in hand, she'd present the information to Nicholas and later Philippe. It'd be an uphill battle with the king; as for Nicholas, she knew he'd be in favor of anything that would help his father live a healthier, happier life. And she'd trust him to do whatever necessary to accomplish the impossible. But could she trust him with her heart ever again after the way they parted in the past? Isabelle wasn't sure she could adequately give an honest answer. Only time would tell if she'd ever be able to open her heart to him again.

The last thing she wanted was to be in Nicholas's debt. She wasn't a miracle worker just because Philippe was smiling, eating a healthy lunch, and seeming to enjoy every minute of it. As Isabelle knew from the notes in the medical file, convincing him to have the surgery would be a feat all its own.

*

Long after his father had gone to bed, Nicholas stood on the balcony outside his own suite, staring into the darkened night at the ocean, to the waves rolling gently to the shore. His thoughts as scattered as the gulls that swooped low over the water in search of food. He stared down at the invitation in his hand, before wadding it up and squeezing his fingers around it.

His ten-year college reunion.

It was the last thing he expected and yet its arrival brought a wealth of emotions. Under normal circumstances he wouldn't have given the paper a second thought but today... Upon opening the small square card, his first thought was he would attend, taking Isabelle. Then realization caught him hard in the solar plexus: that was exactly what he couldn't do. His duty was here, not in the States drinking and reliving old times with people who didn't even know the real him.

He closed his eyes as the guilt washed over him, seeping into every pore, threatening to smother him. It was thirteen long years; but Nicholas remembered the day as if it were yesterday. Pleading his case to his parents, arguing as to why he should be allowed to go to the States to study instead of at the local university. In the end, he'd gotten what he wanted, his mother helping sway his father's decision. A chance to blend in and live a life that didn't include servant's anticipating his every need.

The opportunity led him to Georgetown and Isabelle. Two of the best things he'd gotten from his time in the States. When word reached his ears of his mother's illness, where had he been? Far away with no hope of returning in time for one last chance to speak with his mother. To tell her how much he loved her, enlighten her to his life off the island, and tell her he had gotten the opportunity to train under the finest surgeon. But it was not to be. Instead, he returned home to turmoil, to chaos, and to a family who no longer knew how to function.

He would have gladly bargained with the devil in order to save his mother, selling his soul to make everything right once more.

Nicholas looked down at his hands. For all his training and skills, he couldn't save her and the knowledge tore deep into his soul. He ground his palms into the rough concrete of the railing, the pain nothing compared to how his heart ached even all this time later. If only he hadn't been so bull-headed in wanting his own way, his own life, and his own chance at happiness.

Chapter Six

Isabelle relished her newfound freedom with trips into the village of Wellfleet Isle. She familiarized herself with the people, the unique shops, and the eateries. But what she really enjoyed was time spent with Nicholas seeing what his life had been like since returning to Wellfleet Isle. The ache that gnawed at her fisted itself deep in her chest as Isabelle fought to put the past behind her. No matter how hard she tried, it was always there, reminding her of how truly alone she'd been that night. And nothing would ever change that fact.

It was as though she was a challenge to Nicholas as he tried to wear down her resolve. She steeled herself to his charm, believing she could hold her own against his sexy smile and devilishly good looks. But every time he smiled at her, the armor around her heart would weaken a tiny bit. Every time he touched her hand, she found herself reliving the touch for hours. Worse yet, every time he leaned close, she wished he would kiss her again.

After a while, Isabelle gave up trying and let herself enjoy the sights Nicholas showed her of his homeland. All the while reminding herself the six months would draw to a close and she'd go back to her safe, normal life. A life that didn't include Nicholas Corsairs, heir to the throne of Wellfleet Isle.

"Ready?"

Isabelle spun around to find Nicholas striding toward her, picnic basket in hand and two bodyguards trailing in his wake.

"Yes." She wiped her hands down the sides of her shorts and crossed the terrace toward him. They were to visit the far side of the island so Isabelle could see the rock formations that had stood like silent sentinels for hundreds of years protecting the island from bad weather.

Nicholas motioned to a bright red convertible parked on the long driveway. "I thought it might be nice if we drove ourselves. That way we can chat uninterrupted."

It wasn't like Nicholas to suggest driving separately and part of her want to disagree with him. She looked back at the bodyguards standing a few feet away. "What about your bodyguards? Aren't they coming along?"

"They will follow in the sedan at a discreet distance behind us, until needed."

From what she'd seen on the island so far, they were never needed. Though Isabelle knew they could be called into play at any moment for their service.

"Shall we?" Nicholas pressed his hand to the small of her back, steering her toward the car and opening the door.

"Of course." Isabelle fought down the shiver that started in her toes and quickly worked its way to the top of her head at the mere touch of his skin to hers. She settled herself on the leather seat already warm from the sun and fastened her seat belt, forcing herself to concentrate on the empty road ahead of the car.

Isabelle leaned her head on the headrest and closed her eyes, letting the breeze caress her skin. That was one thing she would definitely miss when she left.

Nicholas's deep chuckle reached her ears and Isabelle opened her eyes to find him staring at her.

"What?"

He shook his head, the smile still playing about his mouth. "You do realize you tend to make noises?"

Isabelle sat straight up, all thoughts of relaxing now pushed from her head. "I most certainly do not."

Nicholas leaned over and tucked a wayward curl that escaped her ponytail back behind her ear. "I must disagree. You looked so peaceful sitting there then you made the most becoming little moan. Almost reminiscent of the weekend at that quaint little

B&B in the Catskills and…" His words trailed off as he quickly averted his gaze back to the road.

Her skin sizzled from his brief touch and her stomach gave a sickening lurch as Isabelle mentally finished the sentence. When they were nestled together in the big comfy bed waiting for the snow to let up. He pulled her to him and kissed her neck, eliciting sounds of passion from her lips. And she welcomed him deep within her body, granting him access to her most private places. Those days were long gone but the memories were hard to forget. Lately Isabelle found herself not wanting to forget. Instead, she wanted to remember each and every second. Except for one…

No, she wouldn't allow herself to go there. Suddenly, being alone with Nicholas seemed like a very bad idea. But it was too late to doing anything about it, short of jumping out of the car and walking back to the palace. She'd have to be on her guard when it came to the man beside her.

*

Nicholas gripped the steering wheel hard, his gaze firmly fastened on the road. The soft groan that escaped Isabelle's lips came close to being his undoing. If they'd been parked, he would have pulled her soft, supple body across the car console onto his lap and kissed her senseless. Heaven only knew what other things he would have done if she encouraged him the slightest bit. Then again, traveling on the narrow mountain road, maybe it better he didn't think of what was to be. Otherwise, they might not live to enjoy the opportunity.

He fought down the hint of guilt that was currently wrapping itself around his brain. He should be at work, readying the hospital for the upcoming Easter Egg Hunt, finalizing the opening ceremony for the maternity wing. His mind should be occupied with balance sheets, contracts, meetings; doing anything but what he was presently doing. Every time the brass ring came around affording him a chance at being normal, Nicholas leaped for it and today was no exception. How long had it been since he'd come to the beach to relax, enjoy the scenery and solitude? Too long, Nicholas told himself, forcing the feelings to the far recesses of his mind. Besides, it was only one day.

Sneaking a quick glance across the front seat of the car, Nicholas noticed Isabelle now sitting ramrod straight, hands folded tightly in her lap. A smile tugged at his lips as he took in her prim and proper stance. So she was as affected by the memory as he was. Yet the knowledge did nothing to soothe the fire in his lower anatomy.

It felt good to be behind the wheel of a car again, his hands wrapped around the leather steering wheel. He felt in control of something in his life for a change. A few minutes later, Nicholas pulled the car off the road and onto a two-track packed dirt path, his bodyguards following behind. At least now his mind would be occupied with keeping the car out of the ruts and not on Isabelle's warm, lush body seated next to him. Though with every jostle of the car against the ground, her breasts jiggled up and down under her t-shirt, destroying any hope of calm. Nicholas ground his teeth and focused on the view outside the windshield.

"We have arrived." Nicholas put the car in park and set the brake. Opening his door, he walked around the vehicle to open Isabelle's door. Before he could even reach the handle, she jumped from the car and was walking across the sand.

"Oh my goodness, this is spectacular. I've never seen anything like it."

Nicholas spread the large blanket on the sand, opened the picnic basket, and retrieved containers of cheese, fruit, and bottles of chilled sparkling water all the while watching Isabelle walk back and forth at the water's edge. Her bright pink toes constantly drew his attention.

"This is one of my favorite places to come when I am in need of solace. It helps me think when there is nothing but the sound of waves against the shore. The rock formations protect the beach from the harsher elements of nature; though the water itself has done quite a bit of damage as you can see." He motioned down the beach to the rocky outcroppings new to the beach over the past few years.

"It's still an incredibly beautiful place. I see why you like it so much. It has a feel to it, hard to describe, but definitely welcoming for anyone needing comfort." She made her way to the blanket.

Isabelle expressed everything that was in Nicholas's heart regarding the beach. As though she knew the words and lifted them from his soul, as if ten years didn't stretch between them. The way her eyes lit up as she watched at the incoming waves, the way her breath hitched in her chest as she inhaled the salty air, and the way she smiled at him.

"You must allow yourself to enjoy what life has to offer. Walk on the beach, kick at the incoming waves, and reach for the brass ring whenever it is within your grasp. Otherwise life will pass you by as you watch from the sidelines."

"Do you practice what you preach?"

"I beg your pardon," Nicholas was confused at her words.

"I haven't seen you walk on the beach or kick the waves." She popped a piece of cheese into her mouth.

"Ah, I see what you are alluding to now." He stood, tugging Isabelle along with him, the feel of her hand warm within his own.

"What are you doing?" She tried to dig her heels into the sand.

"I'm going to walk on the beach, down to the water's edge and kick at the waves. And you will do the same."

Isabelle shook her head. "No, I'm fine up here."

"But I insist." Nicholas swung her up in his arms and threw her over his shoulder. Her laughter rang in his ears as she playfully slapped him on the back.

"Put me down Nicholas. I'm too heavy and you're going to drop me."

"You're not heavy. In fact," he bounced her up and down. "You could stand to gain a few pounds. As for putting you down, I will shortly." He strode purposely toward the water, not stopping until the waves lapped at his calves. Nicholas pulled Isabelle from his shoulder, letting her body slide down the length of him, feeling the swell of her breasts against his torso, her pebbled nipples pressed to his skin. It was all he could not to hold her tight to his body, letting her feel how much she affected him.

He heard the swift intake of her breath as her bare feet came in contact with the cool water and shifted his thoughts reluctantly away from forbidden territory.

"Now Doctor Tandori, kick at the waves. See if you can disperse them with your feet."

She looked confused for a minute, and then turned a brilliant smile on him before taking her foot and sideswiping a wave, drenching Nicholas from knees to ankles with the water. "Like this, your highness?"

Nicholas looked down at his sodden trousers before responding. While she'd done exactly as he'd asked, this wasn't what he'd intended.

He formulated his own plan of attack. "Yes, but this is more in tune with what I meant." He leaned forward, cupped a handful of the water in his palms and tossed it across the front of her t-shirt.

Isabelle let out a yell and immediately went into retaliation mode. Within minutes, they were soaked to the skin and out of breath, laughing at their own antics.

Grabbing her hand, Nicholas led her back up the beach to the blanket. He lowered himself to the ground and pulled his shirt over his head, dabbing at his chest with the soggy garment. After drying himself as best he could, Nicholas dropped the shirt and turned to face Isabelle.

His gaze froze on her chest. The white t-shirt soaked to nearly sheer, outlining her lacy bra as though it had been painted on. Beyond that, her nipples were hard and tight against the wet cotton, every curve clearly accentuated through the thin material. She shivered and Nicholas knew he was a goner.

"Isabelle." Her name a mere whisper from his lips. He couldn't wait, not a minute longer. Nicholas tugged her across the blanket and onto his lap. The feel of her wet t-shirt did nothing to cool the heat in his body at her nearness.

This close he saw the flecks of gold in her eyes and the flame of desire residing within. The notion that Isabelle wanted him as he did her should have sent warning bells to clang in his brain, but didn't. Instead it fueled the fire, urging him forward. He wanted her and needed her, no matter how hard he tried to fight the notion.

Nicholas threw caution to the wind and lowered his mouth to hers, capturing her lips in a blistering kiss. Her soft sigh sent blood pooling straight to his groin and Nicholas buried his hands in her damp hair, pulling her close, angling her head for better access to her mouth. He coaxed her lips open with his tongue, dipping inside to taste the far recesses of her mouth.

Nicholas deepened the kiss. He'd wanted to do this since the moment he'd seen her again. A wave of sexual awareness raced through him, so powerfully strong that Nicholas knew Isabelle felt it as well. She kissed him back without reservation, feeding the flames until Nicholas thought he would explode from wanting.

How he missed Isabelle and having her in his arms brought the feelings to the forefront. Nicholas slipped his hands under the back of her t-shirt, up the warmth of her skin to her bra. Moving his hands to the front of her chest, he cupped her breasts, slowly caressing them, taking his time to relish the feel of her skin beneath his fingers. Nicholas dipped his thumbs inside the edges of the wet lace, stroking her nipples, eliciting another groan from her lips as she surged forward into his touch. He lifted the weight of her breasts, feeling them fill his hands.

Isabelle's hands slipped across his bare skin, over his hardened nipples. It was all he could do not to toss her down on the blanket and have his way with her right here and now. He would start with her pink painted toes, press a kiss to each one in turn, and then leisurely make his way up her body.

Her hands roamed further over his flesh and Nicholas relished her tentative touch. He felt her growing hunger, inciting his body to an even more fevered pitch. Shifting on the blanket, Nicholas fought for control as Isabelle wiggled mercilessly on his lap, pressing herself tight to his rock hard erection. If she kept this up, he would end up embarrassing himself right here and Nicholas didn't want that to happen.

She gave as good as she received, feeling her fingers tunneling through his hair, scraping across his scalp, tugging him closer. He needed her beneath him on the blanket, her arms wrapped around him, her eyes swimming with need, her body burning for his touch as he buried himself within her body. Bunching a handful of the t-shirt material in his fists, he made to lift the garment from her body.

Somewhere through the fog that surrounded his head, Nicholas heard someone clear their throat. Then heard it again and reluctantly pulled back from Isabelle's luscious mouth.

"Pardon the intrusion, your highness."

Isabelle instantly stilled in his arms, her body frozen in place as she tore her lips from his and buried her head in his neck.

"This better be good." Nicholas struggled to get his ragged breathing back under control, his forehead resting against the side of Isabelle's face. "What is it, Andre?"

"I have word from the palace that Prince Aidan has arrived."

It was as though a bucket of ice-cold water had been thrown over his body, dousing the fire that raged only seconds before. Nicholas lifted his head and sent a silent curse skyward.

Realization of where they were and what they were doing slammed into him. What the hell had he been thinking to let his lust for Isabelle take possession of his body? The notion that this was what Nicolas deserved for thinking to slip away for a day didn't escape his notice.

Nicholas set Isabelle from his lap and stood, grabbing his wet shirt and tugging it quickly over his head. A look of confusion and disappointment marred her face, her lips dewy and swollen from his kisses, the flush of arousal still evident on her cheeks and the disheveled clothing made it difficult to do what he had to do at that moment.

He held out his hand to Isabelle. "We must go."

*

Isabelle watched the change come over Nicholas at the mention of his brother's name. Adjusting her clothes and smoothing down the front of her t-shirt, she snuck a peek at him across the front seat of the convertible. Ever since the guard said his brother Aiden arrived, it was as if Nicholas were a different person. Gone was the man who only moments before was kissing her senseless. In his place sat a man with tousled hair, a square jaw resolutely set, and lips thinned to a tight grim line, intent on reaching the palace. It was impossible to know what he was thinking and Isabelle thought it best not to ask.

Only minutes before, Nicholas made her feel alive and vivacious, forgetting her troubles and thinking of nothing but the feel of his body pressed to hers, the warmth of his lips on her mouth, and the taste of his tongue tangling with hers. She wrapped her arms around her middle, hugging herself tightly, feeling the dampness of the shirt against her skin. Even though the sun shone brightly overhead and the warm breeze filled the car, it did nothing to relieve the chill Isabelle now felt or the goosebumps suddenly dotting her flesh. She stared out the window as they drove through town and away from the carefree afternoon. Whatever happened on the beach was now forgotten in Nicholas's haste to return home.

"You'll forgive my abandoning you so abruptly once we return to the palace. I'll need to speak with my brother upon our arrival."

"Of course, I wouldn't expect less," Isabelle replied, trying to finger comb her hair in some semblance of order. Duty took priority over pleasure as Isabelle saw earlier.

As soon as the convertible came to a halt outside the front doors of the palace, Isabelle opened her door and climbed out without waiting for Nicholas or the bodyguard to assist her. She clutched her soaked tennis shoes tightly to her chest in a valiant effort to hide the transparency of her t-shirt from view. The last thing she wanted was to face the arriving prince looking the way she did. Her hair hung in wet tangled curls about her face, her cotton t-shirt soaked to the skin, and her shorts felt as if she'd sat in the ocean rather than frolicked at the shoreline.

Nicholas stood silent by the driver's side door, his gaze focused intently on the terrace. Isabelle followed his line of sight and saw a man standing there. Prince Aidan, she assumed.

"Thank you for a lovely afternoon, Nicholas. If you'll excuse me, I'm going to my room now. I'll check on your father as well."

Nicholas barely dropped a nod in her direction. "As you wish," he murmured distractedly, as though realizing an answer was in order.

The formal tone of voice was back, the rigid stance of his body, and the royal mask firmly in place on his face. Isabelle bit her lip, and then walked toward the front doors of the palace. Right now, nothing she could say or do would penetrate whatever clouded his thoughts.

If only the guard hadn't approached and hadn't brought everything crashing down around them in one fell swoop. She would have loved to run her fingers across his brow, smooth the worry lines, and tell Nicholas everything would be all right. But she couldn't do it. With a heavy heart, Isabelle found herself reliving the day ten years ago waiting for Nicholas to say "Surprise, all a joke, I'm not going anywhere."

His face remained impassive to her fears and anguish as he walked out the door, away from Isabelle and their unborn child.

Just as he did right now.

She wanted him to flash that devilish grin at her, haul her back into his arms and forget everything else. But whatever cosmic forces aligned allowing them to come together for one glorious afternoon was now propelling them apart. Things had quickly gone back to their original status where she was the doctor caring for the king and Nicholas was the prince.

She paused and looked back at Nicholas now striding across the balcony, headed for Prince Aidan. Maybe it was better their lives turned out the way they did. Isabelle shook her head and headed toward her suite. She couldn't imagine being at someone's beck and call twenty-four hours a day, seven days a week. Her steps faltered as she stopped in the middle of the hallway. But that was exactly what she'd done by agreeing to a round-the-clock, six-month commitment to King Philippe. Before that, she'd allowed her own job to consume her life. Every waking moment spent at work, caring for patients, performing surgeries. Not that Isabelle didn't love every minute of it, yet over time, her work became the only thing she did. Being a top-notch surgeon was the only thing she dreamt of for so many years and she had been over-the-moon excited when she achieved her goal. She loved her patients and helping them recover from their heart problems. But at the same time, after experiencing the freedom she felt here on Wellfleet Isle, the thought of going back to her position at Garner General Hospital was making her question her own priorities.

With a rueful sigh, Isabelle pushed opened the door of her suite and closed it behind her. She was no different from Nicholas after all. But she was. Isabelle could walk away from the demands at any time. All she had to do was quit. Looking back at the three years she'd lived with Nicholas, everything had been a farce. A neat and tidy façade concocted to conceal his true identity from everyone, including her. Now the demands on his time were such he couldn't even spend an afternoon away without being called back for one reason or another. It was no way to spend a life, at least not in her opinion. Nicholas had no choice but to stay and do as expected of him, born to the title. And for that, Isabelle felt incredibly sorry for the man who had turned her life royally upside down.

*

After a quick shower and a change of clothes, Isabelle headed to Philippe's suite for her afternoon check-in. She conferred briefly with Denton before turning her attention to Philippe.

Isabelle tried to conceal her frown as she lowered the stethoscope and glanced at the portable blood pressure machine digital readout. The numbers were not where she'd hoped they'd be. "How do you feel?"

"As though I'm an old man with even older body parts, which I'm sure that contraption already tells you. Why do you ask?" Philippe smiled at her, his face pale and wan.

Isabelle shook her head and smiled back at him, not willing to divulge the real reason behind her question. "Are you having any trouble breathing today?"

"I find today a bit worse than yesterday." His words were punctuated by a cough.

"I'm going to increase your oxygen flow and also put you on some added medication. And we'll rerun the EKG in the morning as well."

"You always want to talk about me, when I'd much rather hear about your outing today," Philippe waved his hand in her direction.

Over the past weeks, she'd caught on quickly to Philippe's attempts to thwart her concern for him. And now it seemed he was getting his information from Denton.

"My day was quite nice. The island is beautiful, though I'm surprised at the lack of access to the far side of Wellfleet Isle." There was no way Isabelle planned to tell him what happened on the beach. The last thing she wanted to reach the king's ears was the fact she and Nicholas were kissing and... Isabelle forced the image from her head; sure the flush was working its way up her cheeks.

Philippe shook his head. "In all the years I can recall, only the main road to town is paved. We've kept the natural beauty of the land as it was, hence the dirt path you drove on today. It was my wedding gift to my wife. She loved going there to sit on the sand and watch the waves. Said it gave her time to reflect and made problems easier to resolve. Did Nicholas tell you his mother used to take the boys there?"

His voice grew fainter and Isabelle could hear the rasp as he spoke. Philippe needed to make a decision and soon as to whether or not he'd undergo a heart transplant.

"No, Nicholas never mentioned it. That's a wonderful wedding present you gave to your wife. I think you're the kindest man I've ever met." With conscious thought, Isabelle leaned over and kissed Philippe's cheek. Suddenly she realized the boundary she crossed, and how many rules of protocol she'd broken with the action, and quickly took a step back. "I'm sorry, that was...that was..."

"Very nice," Philippe finished, passing the glass back to her. "Do you know how long it's been since a beautiful woman has kissed me?"

"I bet you had all the women chasing after you when you were younger."

He offered up a wan smile. "Ah, there were a few. That must be where my younger son Aidan gets it from. Always the ladies' man, that one. I hear he has come home. Have you met him yet?"

Isabelle shook her head. "No, but I caught a glimpse of him when Nicholas and I returned from our outing. I believe he and Aidan were about to have a meeting."

Philippe patted her hand before shooing her off with a smile. "Now, off you go and I'll see you in the morning."

The short conversation had obviously drained his limited supply of energy. He was presenting advanced symptoms, as Isabelle knew he would. Medication was only a temporary deterrent to the encroaching dilemma. The longer surgery was delayed the greater the chance for infection and possible pneumonia, and death. Her meeting with Nicholas after evaluating his father had gone accordingly well. He didn't dispute her findings, didn't argue her course of treatment, and as promised, didn't micro-manage every step she took in relation to his father's care.

While nothing Isabelle instituted had reversed the symptoms of Philippe's damaged heart, Isabelle knew getting Nicholas to accept her findings would be easy, but the hard part would be convincing Philippe. Soon time would be of the essence and if she couldn't convince the king within the next few weeks, Isabelle didn't want to think about the outcome that lay ahead should her attempts fail.

Chapter Seven

Isabelle tossed and turned on the luxurious king-sized bed, the events of the previous day cascading through her mind. She finally pushed the silk bedcovers aside and stood. Her mind whirred with a thousand thoughts, every one of them to do with the king's surgery, if only she could get him to agree. Then there was the one extra thought that didn't have anything to do with Philippe and everything to do with Nicholas.

She actually enjoyed herself and had fun; something Isabelle couldn't recall doing for a very long time. Against her better judgment, Isabelle knew, had they not been interrupted, she would have ended up making love with Nicholas, right there on the beach. Regardless of how she tried to tell herself otherwise, the man managed to slip past her defenses and into her heart once more.

Darn Nicholas for disrupting her life so completely. Even when the man wasn't around, he occupied her thoughts far more than permissible. At all hours of the day and night, he would slip into her mind and remind her of the past.

Leaving her suite and arriving in the main dining room for dinner that evening, Cook relayed the message the brothers were eating in the family suite and would be unavailable to join her. While part of her was happy for the solitude, a small part felt bereft at not being able to meet the younger Prince Aidan. But Isabelle knew she would within time. The rest of the evening passed in silence as Isabelle reviewed her notes before bed. Now, here she was still going over the day.

Shoving her fingers through her already tousled curls, she walked to the balcony doors and opened them, letting in the ocean breeze. The night air was heavily scented with the aroma of hibiscus and Isabelle took a deep breath, cleansing her mind of the troublesome thoughts that plagued her.

She stared over the railing at the massive in-ground pool in the family courtyard below. She'd spent a little time relaxing by the pool, shaded by the large umbrellas, reading books, and sipping iced tea since her arrival. Right now Isabelle could think of nothing better than trailing her fingers through the cool water, staring up at the brightly lit stars in the sky, and letting the sounds of the night soothe her frazzled nerves. Pulling a short robe over her nightgown, Isabelle made her way down the steps to the pool.

After a quick peek to make sure the guards weren't presently patrolling the area, she moved to the side of the pool and sat down. Slipping her legs into the water, Isabelle closed her eyes and let out a sigh. Just another perk of the job she found herself getting quite used to.

*

Nicholas had come out here to think, to put the pieces of his life in some semblance of order, but it was no good. Every time he thought he'd made a decision, another argument brought itself to mind, giving him pause to doubt. Aidan coming home was a good thing and a bad thing. Their father needed both his sons around him, but Aidan was also an unwanted distraction.

How dare he breeze back into their life as though nothing had happened. He hadn't seen Aidan more than once since their mother's funeral a decade ago; when his brother left without a backward glance at the massive amount of responsibility he was leaving in Nicholas's hands. The visit had been a strained affair, to say the least. Maybe it was better that way, Nicholas reasoned. But now Aidan had returned.

Nicholas briefly allowed his thoughts to stray. What if he'd been the second born instead of the first heir to the throne? What if he could have been the one to do with his life as he pleased? And what if he was the one who hadn't been called upon to make a choice that would forever change the rest of his life. The "what ifs" were vile creatures, their presence in his mind forcing Nicholas to think things he didn't want to be thinking. With a resolute shake of his head, he tried to push them away as another sound crossed his senses.

Nicholas kept himself shrouded in the shadows by the cabana, watching Isabelle as she lowered herself to the edge of the pool. The movement allowed her robe to gap, exposing the creamy swell of her cleavage. From his vantage point, Nicholas could see her breasts rise and fall with each breath she took.

He had a clear view down the front of her nightgown as she leaned over the water. A view that set his pulse to pound. Her round, ripe full breasts teased him from a distance, her puckered nipples taut and pressed tight against the silky material, begging to be kissed, suckled, and caressed. Nicholas knew if they hadn't been interrupted at the beach, he would have done exactly that. His erection strained at the front of his swim trunks. He hadn't been able to control his emotions earlier any more than now. As the night breeze washed over him, Nicholas hoped it would cool his heated body. If the truth were known, he was tired of burying how he felt behind a stony façade. Never able to do what he wanted as opposed to what he had to do. Until tonight...

Stepping quietly across the concrete fascia, he drew closer, his gaze never leaving her face. He looked at her, her body fairly glowing in the moonlight. With her eyes closed, blissfully ignorant of the fact she wasn't alone, Isabelle looked like the young girl he'd left behind. The memory of his leaving was something Nicholas tried not to think about, for it brought forth a renewed sense of loss. He hated the way he'd left Isabelle that spring day when word arrived from the palace and he'd been forced to leave without revealing a thing to her. He always meant to go back, yet thanks to Aiden's leaving and his father's illness, time had passed him by. But not anymore. He would find a way to rectify everything.

Her soft sigh drew Nicholas away from his musings as he looked over at her, so serene in the moonlight; eyes closed and head tilted back. Her long tanned legs moved back and forth under the water. The same legs that had been wrapped around his waist, as years before Nicholas made sweet love to Isabelle night after night in their little apartment.

The vision all but consumed him. He wanted her, damn it all. There was no doubt about his intentions. She would end up in his bed; he had only to convince her of the fact.

Isabelle turned, her hand quickly pressed to her chest in surprise. "Oh, I didn't know anyone else was around. Nicholas, you startled me. I thought I was alone."

She tugged the edges of her robe together, clutching the lapels tight, robbing him of the delectable view of her body.

"I apologize for disturbing your solitude. Sleep eludes me and I thought a swim might relax my mind." Nicholas ran his heated gaze over her and realized the folly of his ways by thinking this was safe. He should step away, leave the pool, and go back to his room. But his feet refused to cooperate, instead moving closer to her.

"It appears I have the same malady that affects you. I tried to convince myself it would do the trick, but it isn't working." She swung her legs to the side of the pool and made to stand. "I don't want to disturb your swim, so I'll head back to my room."

"Please stay. I would hate to think I forced you away."

Isabelle stared at him for a minute, and then moved to sit on the chaise lounge. "All right, I'll stay for a few minutes."

An image popped into Nicholas's head of Isabelle in a tiny bikini, emerging from the pool, her body soaking wet, her hair slicked back from her face. The barely there swimsuit created by his imagination clinging to her generous curves, outlining her breasts, taunting him to touch her. Then the vision changed and she was naked and beneath him. He closed his eyes, squeezing them shut, fighting for control over his thoughts, his emotions, and his actions.

"Nicholas?" Her soft, breathy voice reached his ears and he lost the battle. "Are you all right? Is something wrong?"

Reason and reality deserted him in his hour of need. If she knew what he was thinking, she would have slapped his face in anger, Nicholas thought.

*

Isabelle's gaze widened as she watched him close the distance, his bare feet making no sound on the concrete as he strode over to where she sat. The urge to flee rose within her, but she forced herself to stay put the closer he came. Nicholas dropped down beside her on the cushion, his knees bumping hers as he lifted her hand, holding it to his chest. Isabelle could feel his heart beat fast and furious, the touch of his bare skin warm beneath her fingers. She couldn't pull her eyes from the way her fingers tangled in the dark crisp hair that dotted his chest, peeking out from the edges of the opened shirt he wore, trailing lower, disappearing inside the waistband. A low rush of air escaped her lungs at the large bulge in his swim trunks as a shiver raced down her spine, and she quickly raised her gaze back to his face.

"Tell me you don't feel the connection we shared in the past. It's still there after all this time." He held her hand tightly in his.

"I don't," Isabelle wasn't sure whom she was trying to convince, steeling herself against the determined look in his eyes. She fought down the urge to lean into his body, seek out the warmth of his skin; pretend the past was something entirely different than she remembered it to be. But no good would come of the idea.

"You always were a poor liar." His hand came up to caress the side of her neck, his fingers slipping behind her neck to tangle in her hair, tugging her forward.

"Nicholas, I..." She didn't want to do this, all the while knowing it would be foolish to deny what her body was telling her. For a second, her gaze slipped toward the palace, to the darkened rooms, hoping no one was standing there in the darkness watching the two of them. The last thing she wanted was an audience who would report to the king what was happening under his own roof.

"I see it in your eyes. I feel it in the way your pulse pounds against my palm. I tasted it in your kisses earlier. We both want the same thing. We need the same thing. But I won't force you to be with me. The choice is yours."

To be with him.

That was all she ever wanted in life, to be with Nicholas. Isabelle felt powerless pressed close to him, and she tipped her head to meet his heated stare. Nicholas captured her lips with his without giving her a chance to object.

Darn, the man was good. Isabelle's head swam from the touch of his mouth on hers with his mind-boggling kisses. She knew she should push him away, resist his very persuasive charm, and high-tail it back to her suite. Instead, she slid her hands under his shirt, touching the warm hard planes of his back. His muscles bunched beneath her fingers as she raked her nails over his skin, earning her a groan from his lips.

The urgency in his kiss spurred Isabelle onward as Nicholas swung her up in his arms and headed up the stairs toward her suite. He trailed his lips across the outer edge of her ear, and down to the curve of her neck, his teeth nipping at her skin, then salving it with his tongue. All rational thought fled as her heart beat faster in anticipation.

When he reached her suite, Nicholas stopped by the side of the bed before lowering Isabelle to her feet. This time she let herself linger against his frame, feeling his hard erection pressed against her stomach as she slid down the muscled planes of his body. Warm moisture pooled between her legs at the thought of what was to come.

"I want you, Isabelle." His words were low and husky in the semi-darkness. "If this isn't what you want, tell me 'no' right now and I'll leave."

Her need for Nicholas far outweighed her need to say no. "Make love to me, Nicholas," Isabelle whispered, the huskiness of her voice matched his.

He slowly pushed the robe from her shoulders, before lowering his head. She sighed against his mouth, as his fingers slipped under the tiny straps of her nightgown, deftly sliding them down her arms to pool on the carpet below. Her panties quickly followed. The cool night air drifted over her skin before Nicholas wrapped her in his arms, chasing away the cold.

Nicholas lowered her to the bed, covering her body with his, kissing her lips till she was breathless with need.

"You are so beautiful."

Isabelle closed her eyes and reveled in the sensations he was creating within her body. She gasped and arched upward as his mouth found her nipple, sucking on it. Reaching forward, she buried her fingers in his hair, anchoring him to her breast, willing him to continue the delightful torture. "Yes."

He moved lower, trailing kisses across her stomach, dipping in her navel, and then lower still as his stubble gently abraded her thighs, until Isabelle thought she couldn't handle any more.

"Nicholas, please," Isabelle found herself at the point of begging.

With his tongue drawing slow circles over her swollen flesh, Nicholas slid his finger deep inside her, teasing her, toying with her as the tension built between her legs. Isabelle moaned, her head thrashing side to side on the pillows, her fingers buried in the bedcovers as she rode the wave to fulfillment. The world slowly came back into focus as Isabelle opened her eyes to find Nicholas poised above her.

"I don't want to hurt you."

"You won't," Isabelle assured him. She boldly grasped him in her hand, reacquainting herself with his body, rubbing her thumb over the drop of moisture that clung to the tip of him.

Nicholas slid his knee between her thighs and shifted his weight atop her. Isabelle moaned softly as he sheathed himself deeply within her. Her body stretched to accommodate him, a slight ache settling itself within her limbs as she relaxed her muscles, welcoming him inside. Their bodies melded together as if they'd never been apart. They searched for and found the ancient rhythm that set the pace for their unhurried lovemaking, each stroke taking them higher and higher until Isabelle couldn't hold back any longer.

She cried out his name as she tumbled over the edge, taking Nicholas with her. He stiffened in her arms, seeking and finding his own release.

Neither spoke as the sound of their breathing filled the silence of Isabelle's room.

Isabelle rested her head on Nicholas's chest, listening to the steady cadence of his heart under her cheek.

"I knew we would be perfect together. Some things never change." Nicholas wrapped his arm around her waist, tugging her closer, and kissed the top of her head.

He skimmed his fingers over her stomach, inciting the riot within her body anew. Isabelle knew she would deny him nothing at this moment. But when the light of day dawned tomorrow, everything would be different. Right now, all she cared about was the man beside her. She lifted herself on one elbow and stared at his face. Never breaking eye contact, she slid down the length of him and found him hard once more.

"Now it's my turn," she whispered, before settling her body over his, feeling the thick erection press deep between her thighs. "Yes." The words escaped her lips as Nicholas took hold of her hips, gently holding her in place as he thrust upward, filling her body. Stars exploded behind her closed eyelids as Isabelle let the feelings overcome her, minutes later hearing his own hoarse cry as he followed her over the precipice. She needed this, she wanted this, and tonight she would have him.

*

Nicholas tightened his hold on Isabelle's waist, tugging her closer to his body. He wanted to wrap her in his arms and never let her go. Their coming together brought back feelings he thought were long gone, memories of a distant past, never to be repeated. How wrong he was with the idea that having her in his bed would change everything. It had done the exact opposite. After making love with her, Nicholas knew one night would never be enough to sate his need for Isabelle. He needed to find a way to make her stay long after his father returned to good health.

Making love to Isabelle had recharged his body, energized his soul and brought to light the knowledge he would never be able to have her. Knowing how much he'd hurt her with his past actions warred within him, blending then and now together for a brief second. But the woman who lay naked and cuddled close beside him knew exactly who he was. The same man, yet not the same. Even though Isabelle's lips responded to his kisses, her body to his eager touch, she held something in reserve. Nicholas wasn't sure how he knew this, but it was there.

No words were necessary nor given as they lay with bodies tangled and fingers entwined on the bed. If he were to speak, Nicholas wasn't sure what he would say. He waited until the sound of her breathing evened out, her body now pliant and warm in his arms. The moonlight lit her face with a soft glow and Nicholas studied her sleeping peacefully beside him. Watched the rise and fall of her creamy full breasts, barely concealed by the silk bed sheets. Breasts he knew fit perfectly in the palms of his hand, dusky nipples that hardened instantly beneath his touch, his lips, and lower still, silky thighs that welcomed him between them.

The black of night slowly faded, leaving in its place the rose-hued colors of dawn. Nicholas slowly moved from the bed knowing he needed to return to his own suite. He didn't relish the idea of anyone seeing him leave her rooms in the early morning light and at the same time hated the idea of leaving her to awaken without him beside her. He needed to maintain his dignity as well as hers. If anyone were to find him in her bed, it would be difficult, let alone impossible, to explain their affair. Though the word sounded illicit and dirty, Nicholas could find no other way to describe it.

Tugging on his damp swim trunks, Nicholas paused beside the bed. Isabelle was curled into a tight ball, her hand tucked under her chin as she slept on blissfully unaware of his scrutiny. The rosy flush still visible on her cheeks, the rasp of his whiskers leaving a hint of abrasion on her neck, the scent of their lovemaking still clinging to the bed sheets and his skin. What he would have preferred was to climb back under the covers, take her in his arms and make love to her again before the sunrise found its way into the room. But he must not; he could not. Instead, Nicholas dropped a soft kiss on the top of Isabelle's head and slipped out through the balcony doors.

*

Isabelle came awake slowly in the bright light of day. The sun streamed through the closed balcony doors. She gnawed at her bottom lip; positive the doors were open last night after Nicholas… Her train of thought trailed off as Isabelle remembered with utmost clarity what happened in this very room the night before. Right here in her bed for that matter.

She looked down at herself, naked under the covers. Casting her gaze sideways, she glanced to the opposite side of the bed, not sure what she would find. The bed was empty, save for her. When Nicholas left, Isabelle wasn't quite sure. But she knew it was for the best. A combination of relief and sadness filled her. She rolled over, burying her face in the soft pillow, inhaling the lingering scent of Nicholas's cologne, letting the fragrance tickle her senses. Running her hand across the silken sheets where he'd previously lain, she allowed her mind to wander.

In the first few months after Nicholas left so abruptly many years before, Isabelle found herself lying awake at night, her hand caressing the cold, empty side of the bed he once slept on. She'd never been able to forget the violent shudders that racked her body as the tears fell in the dark for no one to see, his pillow tucked tightly under her cheek. The pain of knowing she was truly alone. She pulled herself together enough to get to class, going through the motions, answering at the appropriate times, doing what was necessary to graduate. Then she packed up her belongings and left town, never looking back.

She'd gone on a few dates when the loneliness all but consumed her. Isabelle stopped trying to find someone to wile away the hours with, stopped trying to replace Nicholas, and stopped trying to convince herself she really didn't care one way or another about the past.

Throughout the years, she'd catch a glimpse of someone with Nicholas's features and wonder if she ever crossed his mind after all these years. Now, Isabelle knew the answer. Their lovemaking awakened a need she thought was long dead and buried. Apparently, she'd thought wrong.

With a laugh, Isabelle pushed back the covers and stood, then made her way into the bathroom. Her hair a mess of tangled curls, her lips swollen and dewy, but it was the tiny dots of red on her breasts that caused her eyes to widen in the mirror above the vanity. Isabelle touched her fingers to the spot then quickly dropped them remembering how the marks had been made.

Nicholas's lips on her skin were the culprits and she wouldn't have wished it any other way.

"Oh my goodness." The words came out soft and breathy.

She looked like a woman who'd been sufficiently loved, which she had been over the course of the previous night. Memories she could file away for future reference while never truly forgetting the events of the past.

Chapter Eight

Isabelle fairly floated down the steps from her suite to the main level of the palace, her thoughts to the point of giddy as she relived the previous night spent in Nicholas's arms. Smiling at the guard in the hallway, she came to a stop just outside the main dining room doors. The sound of raised voices from within caused her to pause momentarily before entering. She debated going in, not wanting to intrude on what was so obviously a personal conversation. One voice she could recognize, the other was unfamiliar.

"I don't care to discuss what you've been doing for the past ten years. All I want to know is when you plan to stop the partying and paparazzi-fest you have so eagerly embraced since you walked out that door after Mother's funeral."

"Why does it matter to you what I do?"

Isabelle knew without a doubt the other voice belonged to Prince Aidan.

"Because I'm tired of cleaning up after you, making excuses to the people of Wellfleet about why you don't come home, and more so making excuses to father when he asks when you will be returning."

"Then it's a lucky thing I showed up when I did, isn't it? You won't have to tell him anything. I'll fill him in myself." The sound of silverware clattering to the tabletop filled the air.

"I'm warning you, Aidan, if you upset him in any way, I'll…" The words trailed off as Nicholas caught sight of Isabelle in the doorway.

"Good morning, Isabelle."

"Nicholas," she dropped a nod in his direction, trying to keep her voice neutral as she walked into the room.

Aidan quickly moved from his chair and approached Isabelle. "Good morning, I don't believe I've had the pleasure of an introduction, for if we had, I'm quite positive I would have remembered someone as lovely as you. I'm Aidan Corsairs, younger brother of Prince Nicholas over there. The one with the grumpy attitude going on at the far end of the breakfast table."

"Good morning. I'm Isabelle Tandori, the doctor caring for your father."

"Ah, so you're the one everyone is talking about. Hey doc, I think I have a hangnail." The younger man held out his hand to Isabelle. "What would you suggest I do about it?"

"Put on a bandage and get over it." The man was a definite charmer.

Aidan pressed his hand over his heart in mock sadness, as he feigned heartbreak. "Ouch, you mortally wound me, my dear lady."

"And I'm very certain you'll find a way to get over my callous bedside manner." His lighthearted manner and irascible way were a direct contrast to the angry words Isabelle heard minutes earlier.

The younger prince threw back his head and laughed aloud. "You know, if all doctors' looked like you, I'd feel the need to get sick more often."

"I'll take that as a compliment." Isabelle smiled at Aidan. He was definitely a ladies' man, a flirt, and decidedly harmless.

Aidan bowed low over her hand, brushing her skin with his lips.

There was no doubt Nicholas and Aidan were brothers. Both were tall with dark wavy hair, vivid and captivating blue eyes, and similar muscular bodies that could turn a woman's head within seconds. And probably had many times, Isabelle thought.

But that's where the similarities ended. Their personalities put them in direct opposition to one another. Whereas Nicholas was more brooding, prone to moments of serious reflection and all business, Aidan was light and fun, quick to smile, laugh aloud without fear of who heard him. The argument she'd interrupted clearly wasn't finished and Isabelle knew Nicholas wouldn't continue it while in her presence.

"Nicholas, if you have no objections, I'd like to visit the hospital today and have a look at the surgery suite after I check in on your father."

Nicholas looked down at his watch. "I have a meeting there at eleven this morning. If you'd like, we could ride in together."

Isabelle nodded. That would be the perfect opportunity for them to spend more time alone she thought, trying not to get her hopes up. "Yes, that would be wonderful. I'll be ready."

"You know, I'd like to join you as well. It's been a while since I've been inside the hospital." Aidan spoke up, lowering his coffee cup to the table.

Nicholas nodded. "Very well, I'll meet you both in the front foyer at ten-thirty."

*

Nicholas tried to concentrate on his breakfast, but it was of no use. Setting the fork on the half-filled plate, he watched his younger brother's boyish antics with Isabelle. The way Aidan repeatedly fawned over her, touching her hand every chance he could, leaning toward her without reason, being overly attentive to the point of obnoxious caused Nicholas to ball his hands into fists at his sides, surprised at the way he felt. It was his brother, for heaven's sake.

But it was whom his brother was kissing that made his blood boil.

Isabelle.

Had it have been any other woman, Nicholas wouldn't have given it a second thought. If anyone was to be kissing her, it should have been him. She was his woman.

The intensely powerful show of emotion startled him. He was jealous. Jealous of his brother's carefree attitude toward life. Jealous of the fact Aidan wasn't responsible for anyone but himself. And jealous of the fact that Nicholas had only been able to live that same lifestyle for a short while, before being called back into family service here on Wellfleet Isle.

The sound of Isabelle's laughter floated past his ears as she laughed at something Aidan said. Nicholas tossed his napkin on the table, pushed back his chair, and stood. He needed to get out of the dining room and away from the two of them before he did something most un-royal, like deck his own brother.

*

"You really don't have to go with me. I'm perfectly capable of doing this on my own." Isabelle argued, though deep inside, she was thrilled with the thought of spending the day with Nicholas.

"I want to go with you. I enjoy spending time with you and today my schedule is light enough I can arrange for a few hours off."

Isabelle stood on the main street of town, trying to figure out where to start. She took a few steps in one direction, and then paused before heading in another.

The sound of Nicholas's laughter rang in her ears. It was wonderful to hear him laugh and she knew she'd never tire of the sound. He should do it more often, Isabelle thought.

"If you'd like, go in every shop. Then you won't miss anything." Isabelle gnawed on her lip. "Are you sure you won't mind?"

Nicholas shook his head and closed the distance between them. "If it means spending more time with you, then it's a good thing." He opened to the door to the bakery and ushered Isabelle inside.

"How will I ever choose?" Isabelle looked around at all the choices, her mouth watering with each and every one.

"Don't choose. Buy one of each pastry."

"I can't, I'd be big as a house."

The long, slow sweep of his eyes over her body had Isabelle squirming in her sandals. She forced herself to look away to keep the flush currently heating her body from becoming an all-out attack on her senses.

"Even big as a house, I can think of many pleasurable things we could do together." The words were spoken low, next to her ear as Nicholas leaned around her, his shoulder grazing the edge of her breast as he reached for a sample of the apple pie, and Isabelle felt her nipples harden instantly.

Isabelle wandered in and out of the shops, each one causing a bigger dent in her wallet. She asked Nicholas his opinion, then ignored his reasoning and did as she pleased. It was refreshing to have the old Nicholas by her side. The one who egged her on to buy something she'd never use, but would treasure the memories it carried because of when it was purchased.

"I think this would make a wonderful addition to your reference library," he said, holding up a book. "Of course I'd be willing to offer my services."

Isabelle glanced at the page, and then hurried over to quickly close the cover before anyone else saw the erotic illustrations.

"Put that down," she hissed, trying to grab the book from his hands. "What are you thinking?"

He grinned at her, and Isabelle found herself drawn to his lips, the book of sexual positions almost forgotten.

"I was thinking of how much fun it might be to recreate the poses on the pages." He lifted an eyebrow suggestively.

Isabelle gulped. This was the man she'd fallen in love with, the one who could make her forget everything else and just live. In the end, Isabelle bought the leather-bound book, much to Nicholas's approval.

"Page one-forty-three. Meet me at the pool cabana at midnight."

With a laugh, she playfully punched him on the arm. "In your dreams, your highness."

Nicholas shook his head. "No, definitely while I'm awake."

He continued his assault on her senses all day. Touching her arm when no one was looking, purposely rubbing his body against her while squeezing past her in the aisles, making sexy, sultry comments in each shop until Isabelle was forced to cut her trip short for fear of throwing herself at the man and begging him to make love to her right on the shop floor.

*

"Shall we?" Nicholas hauled her atop his lap in the limousine for a deep, blistering kiss, his hands cupping her breasts, his fingers stroking her hardened nipples. Just one touch from the man made her insides melt into a puddle of mush. She'd gone willingly into his embrace, needing to feel his body on hers. The world outside faded as Isabelle sought relief within his arms. If every day could be like this, she thought.

"So what did you think of the surgical facilities for the cardiac unit?"

"Very impressive. You've done a fabulous job with bringing the most up-to-date equipment to the hospital. The staff was very knowledgeable."

How could he keep his mind on business at a time like this? It was all she could do to coherently answer his question while his fingers danced their way over her skin.

"It's important that the people who live on the island have the best medical care within reach." Nicholas was undoing the buttons on her blouse, his hands separating the front of the material. "This way they don't have to wait to be flown off the island for urgent care."

"Nicholas, what are you doing?"

"Something I haven't been able to do all day."

"And that is? Oh…" Her eyes drifted shut as his mouth found her breast. Isabelle grabbed his shoulders for support as Nicholas teased her willing flesh, drawing the tight bud of her nipple into his mouth. The man was insatiable and Isabelle wouldn't have it any other way.

She felt his hands slip down her back, caressing every inch of her body until he reached the hem of her skirt. He bunched the material in his hands, trailing his fingers over the back of her thighs, higher until he found what he was searching for and exactly what she needed.

A hiss of air came from Isabelle's parted lips. "Nicholas, please."

"What would you have me do? This?" He stroked the moist flesh between her legs, his fingers dipping inside, tormenting her with every touch.

Isabelle molded herself to his body until she didn't know where she ended and Nicholas began.

"Yes, do that. Harder." Her words more frantic as the motion of his fingers increased. Isabelle rocked her hips against his hand, soft whimpers escaping her mouth.

"As you wish."

He slipped one finger inside her, then two. Isabelle felt her body tighten as she arched her back, spiraling out of control in his arms, stars exploding before her closed eyelids.

She came back to reality in his arms, her face buried against his shoulder, the aftershocks still rippling through her body.

After a few minutes, Isabelle lifted her head. "I've never made love in a limo. It was quite nice."

"Quite nice is for Sunday strolls in the park. Making love in a limo is definitely better than that."

"Maybe you should show me again in case I missed something the first time."

"It would be my pleasure."

The look on his face was one of pure determination and Isabelle knew she'd be very satisfied when he was finished. Nicholas lowered his head, capturing her lips beneath his as Isabelle gave herself over to the feelings he created. She didn't ever want the day to end.

*

Nicholas watched Isabelle straighten her clothes, crossing her arms over her chest in an effort to hide her obvious reaction to him. Everything about her drove him crazy with wanting her. He needed to touch her, to taste her, to bury himself within her body. Within minutes, they would be back at the palace, once more ensconced within the walls and everything would be different.

He lifted her hand to his mouth and pressed a lingering kiss to her palm. She smiled at him and he felt his heart skip a beat. Today had been a new experience for him. One he enjoyed immensely and hoped to repeat many times over the course of her stay here.

Isabelle lifted the plain-covered book from the store wrapper and laid it on her lap. With a saucy smile, she opened the cover and rifled through the pages.

"Let's see now. What page was it again that caught your eye?"

Nicholas felt himself harden at the thought of the images on the pages. He removed the book from her hand and tossed it to the seat of the limo. "All of them," were his last words before hauling Isabelle onto his lap once more.

*

Time flew past faster than Isabelle ever imagined it would as she slid her sunglasses over her eyes and smiled happily at the man beside her. Accepting Nicholas's outstretched hand, she allowed him to escort her from the vehicle. Isabelle thought of the evening she had planned for him. Tonight would be the night she'd tell him she loved him, after all this time, after everything they'd been through in the past. Tell him and hope that his feelings ran as deep.

Out on the side lawn, Isabelle watched entranced with the way the children flocked to Nicholas. How effortlessly he slipped into the role of ruler, posing with the hospital staff and the pediatric patients for a photograph, how easily he fit into the image of king, how flawless the transition right before her eyes as Nicholas handled the PR like the well-seasoned pro he was. On her last visit into Wellfleet, she'd toured the cardiac surgery suite, familiarizing herself with the equipment and staff for when the surgery would be performed on King Philippe. She was satisfied everything would be in readiness when the timing was right. For now, all she could hope was that Philippe would change his mind on his own over the next few days and consent.

When they'd left the hospital three weeks earlier, Nicholas announced there would be an Easter Egg Hunt at the hospital for the Easter holidays. Now that the day had arrived, Isabelle was surprised at the turnout. She'd been prepared for something low-key and small. Not the festive party that awaited them as she alighted from the limousine that morning.

Nicholas spoke to each child in turn, calling them by name, asking questions about what they had been doing and how their schooling was going. One by one, until all of the children received his personal welcome. What amazed Isabelle the most was that these were all in-patients at the hospital. Each there for varied illnesses and treatments, and yet the staff made it a priority to ensure the children participated in the age-old tradition of hunting for Easter eggs.

Isabelle watched as a little girl tugged hard on Nicholas's pant leg. He smiled down at her, extended his hand and off they went in search of the multi-colored plastic eggs. As Isabelle watched,

Nicholas dropped to his knees and helped the child search under the bushes, never seeming to care that his pants were getting dirty.

More children came running up, pleading with Nicholas to help them in the search. For a few minutes, the sound of the children laughing and calling to one another filled the air. Then Isabelle heard the unmistakable sound of his rich, deep laugh penetrating the younger voices as they all ran off down the slope of the lawn in front of the hospital.

Nicholas turned, meeting her gaze and smiling at her before returning to the children. Isabelle tried to swallow past the lump in her throat. He would be such a wonderful father; any child would be lucky to have him as a dad. He was so patient and kind, willing to drop everything to help the children find their treat-filled eggs.

She unconsciously lifted her hand to her stomach, and for a minute the image of Nicholas helping their own child search for eggs crossed her mind. Would it be a boy, looking just his father with dark hair and deep blue eyes? Or possibly a little brown-haired girl, dressed in frilly lace and holding her daddy's hand as she searched for the brightly colored plastic eggs. Isabelle closed her eyes and tried to breathe past the ache in her heart. The same kind of father he would have been if their baby had lived ten years ago.

The world tilted crazily and stars swam before Isabelle's eyes. She needed to find someplace quiet to compose herself, but knew it would appear odd if she were to suddenly disappear without a word. Settling herself on a wrought iron park bench, Isabelle decided to remain there for the time being. No one would miss her as they ran to and fro searching for candy.

"Ah ha, there you are."

Isabelle turned to find Aidan striding in her direction, a glass of lemonade in each hand and a newspaper tucked under his arm.

"I figured you might be thirsty." He handed her a glass before sitting down beside her.

"Thank you."

Aidan shook his head. "I'm on duty this afternoon for the storybook hour. How Peter Rabbit got his groove or something like that. I can't quite remember the name of the book."

"I think it's wonderful what Nicholas and you are doing for the children. And I'm sure their parents are thrilled to be able to bring some small amount of joy to what would otherwise be just an ordinary day."

"You shouldn't be giving me so much credit. It certainly isn't warranted or deserved."

"What do you mean? Of course it is." Isabelle took a sip of the lemonade, the cold liquid sliding down her throat.

"This was why I left Wellfleet Isle in the first place. I wanted to be in charge of my own life, my own destiny, and here I can't. Here my needs come lower on the totem pole." Aidan took a sip of his drink before continuing. "And yes, that makes me very self-centered, but that's who I am."

Isabelle shook her head. "No, not self-centered, just very much in control of your own life and there's nothing wrong with that. Nicholas is the eldest son; it was only natural that he assumed the position when your father became ill."

Aidan set the glass on the bench between them. "Did you know he stepped right into the role without hesitation? He never questioned the responsibilities, did it without hesitation as if there were no other course to take. I'm sure it wasn't easy with father pulling away and mother gone… Nicholas had his hands full. I'd just started university and once the funeral was over, I left and never looked back."

His words filtered through her brain, the memory of Nicholas leaving her skittering across her mind. "Aidan, I'm sure Nicholas wouldn't want you to blame yourself for wanting a different life."

He lifted his shoulder in a shrug. "Possibly not. I'm referred to in the press as the 'Playboy Prince' and for very good reason.

Last night, I had a very long talk with Nicholas. I've obtained my license as a Medevac pilot with EMT certification, and my training will allow me to help the people here more than ever. But first and foremost I'm back on Wellfleet to assume whatever duties Nicholas needs of me."

"I'm sure Nicholas couldn't be prouder of you for what you've accomplished."

Aidan threw back his head and laughed, his action knocking both the glass of lemonade and the newspaper off the bench and onto the ground. "Only time will tell, my dear Isabelle. Only time will tell."

Isabelle looked down at the paper on the ground, staring at a picture of herself, though a much younger version. She leaned over and lifted the newspaper, her eyes never leaving the article on the front page as she stared at the headline emblazoned across the top of the page.

The New Royal Triangle—Is the future King of Wellfleet Isle playing doctor on his off-duty hours?

The article talked about her and Nicholas dating in college, living together while attending medical school and Nicholas completing his residency. The picture was of the two of them wrapped in one another's arms at a fraternity party some eleven years prior. She looked so young, so naïve and so in love. A more recent picture was taken when they were shopping in town. The day she tripped on the curb and Nicholas caught her, but that wasn't what the image showed. It showed two people looking only at one another, seeing nothing else, lost in a world of their own. And the reporter picked up on it commenting on Nicholas keeping company with an old flame while awaiting the arrival of a new one. Bile rose in Isabelle's throat as she fought down the urge to lose her breakfast.

Her gaze was drawn to the opposite picture on the page.
The future Princess of Wellfleet Isle, Marissa Sophia VanMeerden.

The knowledge this was the woman who would marry Nicholas made Isabelle feel as though a knife had been plunged into her chest. A proxy engagement made to a woman he'd yet to meet until fall at the official announcement of their engagement party here on Wellfleet. The woman was stunning in a pale green silk ball gown. It was as though she'd stepped directly off the pages of a fashion magazine. A tall slender body, platinum blonde hair and incredibly gorgeous green eyes stared back at Isabelle. Just the type of woman to marry a soon-to-be king.

Her many attributes were spelled out in black and white for the world to see. A royal lineage dating back to King Ferdinand of Spain, she spoke four languages, was beautiful, poised and everything Isabelle wasn't and never would be. Isabelle was plain vanilla ice cream, whereas Marissa was rocky road ice cream with extra marshmallows blended in. The enormity of the situation tore at Isabelle. This was the woman who would be queen and Nicholas had never said a word about her to Isabelle.

The article brought home everything that had been on Isabelle's mind. Why Nicholas never held her hand in public, why he never kissed her when anyone was around, and why he only came to her room in the dark of night. Regardless of what they shared, Isabelle would never be more than a passing fling to Nicholas. Especially since he already had a bride waiting in the wings. Which meant Isabelle was nothing more than the warm-up act. The air left her lungs in a rush as she gasped for breath, and an icy chill passed over her skin leaving her stomach in knots. Her hands shook as the newspaper fell unheeded to the ground at her feet.

Aidan took hold of her hands. "Isabelle, your hands are like ice." He looked down, saw the newspaper, and then looked up at her face.

"I'm fine really. But if you'll excuse me, I'm going to go back to the palace."

She meant to let go of the bench and start walking, but found her legs wouldn't comply with her brain.

"Oh my god, it's the article. You didn't know about Marissa?" Putting his arm around her waist, Aidan moved closer. "Let me help you. The limousine is out front. Shall I alert Nicholas?"

"No!" The words came out sharper than intended. "No, he doesn't need to be disturbed. Let him attend to the children. Don't ruin their day by disturbing them." Allowing Aidan to escort her to the limousine, Isabelle concentrated on putting one foot in front of the other. The last thing she needed was to make a scene. Not here and not now.

"Are you positive you wouldn't like me to let Nicholas know?" Aidan settled her in the limousine, concern still marring his features.

Isabelle shook her head. "No, please don't. Promise me you won't say a word to him. I'll be fine in the morning." But she wouldn't be. She'd never be whole again. Not after today. It was as though all the bright spots in her life had suddenly turned pitch black.

Aidan gave her a thorough once over look before letting out a frustrated sigh. "All right, I'll respect your wishes. But if you still feel this way in the morning, please let me call the doctor for you. I mean…you know what I mean."

"I'll be okay, Aidan. Really, I don't need a doctor. I just need…" Isabelle didn't know what she needed. The tears gathered in her eyes and she quickly brushed them away. She wouldn't cry in front of Aidan, she couldn't. "I've got to go."

He leaned forward and pressed a kiss to her cheek. "I'll drop by in the morning to check on you. Don't do this to yourself, Isabelle. Don't waste another minute of precious energy trying to change what you can't," Aidan implored her.

"Thank you. You're a very kind man, Aidan." She'd barely closed the door when the tears began to fall. She was out of her league. In fact, compared to the woman in the article, Isabelle wasn't anywhere even remotely in the ballpark. Could she have been any stupider? Apparently she could be and was. Isabelle blindly hoped there might be something between them, given the time they'd spent together both in and out of bed was more than just a way to pass the hours. She'd thought wrong on that count as well

Now to find out another woman was already set to assume the role of princess next to Nicholas on the throne, in his bed and in his heart. A woman who'd been in place long before Isabelle even knew Nicholas. Looking back, Isabelle wondered whether Nicholas's leaving her suite in the early morning hours might not be more for the protection of his own image. It wouldn't be wise for the future king to be caught leaving the bed of an employee of the royal household. Think of the scandal it would cause should they be caught. How could she have been so blind not to see what was directly in front of her face? The thought made Isabelle feel physically sick to her stomach and she prayed she'd make it back to her suite in time.

Chapter Nine

Nicholas lifted the coffee cup to his lips seconds before the newspaper landed on his breakfast plate, displacing the food across the linen-covered table and jostling his hold on the cup as the hot liquid splashed onto his lap. He leaped to his feet, blotting at his pants before the coffee had a chance to soak through to his skin and burn him.

"What the hell are you doing?" He directed his confusion toward Aidan, now glaring at him from beside the dining table.

"That's exactly what I was about to ask you. Explain this to me, would you, big brother. For I find I'd very much like to use your face as a punching bag right now." Aidan stalked back and forth across the dining room, his steps agitated, hands clenched into fists by his side.

Nicholas looked down at the paper, seeing the decade-old photograph of himself and Isabelle in Maryland, then the more recent photograph of him and Isabelle. He shoved his hand through his hair as a groan escaped his lips. Sinking back down into the chair, he read the article in its entirety before lifting his gaze to Aidan.

"Has Isabelle seen this?"

"What do you think?"

The look on his brother's face was enough to tell Nicholas everything he needed to know. When he queried the maid as to whether Isabelle would be joining them for breakfast, the response was Doctor Tandori was feeling under the weather. Now Nicholas knew the weather had nothing to do with it. And it explained why his phone calls to her suite had gone unanswered.

"Give me one good reason why I shouldn't deck you right here and now?" Aidan questioned accusingly, his fists raised.

Nicholas shook his head. "I can't think of one at the moment. Have at it." He sat back in the chair and waited for the inevitable right hook to the jaw, but it didn't come. Back when they were younger, Nicholas had bested his brother at every turn in the practice ring. Now from the look on Aidan's face, Nicholas didn't doubt he would come out on the losing end.

Aidan dropped down heavily in the nearest chair. "You should have seen the look on her face when she saw the article yesterday. I thought she knew about Marissa and you. My god man, she was beyond devastated. She doesn't deserve this and most certainly doesn't deserve you."

Nicholas could say nothing to dispute Aidan's words. A sick feeling settled in the pit of his stomach at the thought of the pain he caused her. How she must hate him at present.

"How do you plan on fixing this?" Aidan demanded.

"I don't know that I can. The engagement's been in place since Marissa's birth. According to royal decree, nothing can nullify the proxy." Nicholas looked down at the newspaper, and then folded it in half as if doing so would somehow erase everything on the page.

"Well you better figure something out fast or you're going to lose the best thing that's ever happened to you." With that said Aidan turned on his heel and left the room.

Nicholas picked up the newspaper and began to read. Each word burned into his brain like a dagger. What had he done? How many people had been hurt by the piece? Too many, Nicholas knew without hesitation. There was no doubt Isabelle didn't care if she ever talked to him again. Not that he would have blamed her. He scrubbed his hands over his face. There was no doubt in his mind he'd already lost her.

*

Isabelle's eyes felt gritty from lack of sleep and, worse yet, crying. So far she'd been able to avoid Nicholas quite neatly for the past two days until now, when one of the servants had come to her suite saying Nicholas had asked her to join him in his private office at her earliest convenience. Isabelle knew she couldn't refuse the invitation without arousing suspicion, so she begrudgingly followed the maid. But as soon as the meeting was over, she was off to the king's suite for her last visit of the day.

"His highness will be with you as soon as he finishes his telephone call."

Isabelle smiled at the secretary and took a seat in front of the massive desk, her thoughts jumbled, and her emotions running rampant. Jumping from the chair, she paced back and forth across the large office. The pictures on the wall caught her eye and Isabelle stopped to stare at one in particular, of Nicholas and a very well-known French film actress. She was wearing a barely there dress and was pressed tightly to his side. So tight that Isabelle doubted even a flea could come between them. But it was the predatory look in the woman's eyes that had Isabelle biting her lip at the feeling of jealousy that surged through her veins. She pushed down the notion, reminding herself in no uncertain terms that there was nothing to be jealous about. Nicholas could see whomever he wanted to as was evidenced by his engagement to Marissa what's-her-name. Swinging around, she resumed her pacing.

On her third pass, Isabelle chanced a glance over at Nicholas's desk. Everything was so neat and tidy, the leather blotter free of pens, messages or anything else to clutter it up. The stack of manila file folders piled neatly in the in-box. Isabelle paused, the wording on the edge of one folder drawing her attention.

Doctor Isabelle Tandori.

What exactly was Nicholas doing with a file folder on her? Isabelle reached for the folder and opened it. She scanned the pages, rising anger now replacing her fragile nerves. So intent on reading the words contained within, she failed to hear Nicholas enter the room.

"I apologize for keeping you waiting." He moved further into the room, settling himself in the chair behind the desk.

"You had me investigated." The words came out more of a statement than a question as Isabelle tossed the file on the desk in front of Nicholas. "I hope you found what you were looking for."

Nicholas had the good graces to look almost embarrassed. Almost, Isabelle thought, but seemingly not enough for her satisfaction.

"Not investigated per se, I was..." His words broke off as he replaced the folder on the stack.

"I'm sorry, if not investigated, then what would you call it?" She resumed her agitated pacing across the room.

"I needed to ascertain information on your background in regard to my father's care. Decisions needed to be made. Plans put into place before we could move forward with approaching you."

Isabelle wasn't convinced. "And by my being here these past few months, I can safely assume nothing turned up to be detrimental or a threat to Wellfleet Isle's national security." She dropped down heavily into the chair.

"I didn't ask you here to fight." Nicholas shoved his hand through his hair.

"Why did you want to see me?" Not that it really mattered to Isabelle either way. The fight left her limbs as fatigue took its place. All she wanted was for the day to be over and to be as far away from Nicholas Corsairs as she could get, being stuck on the same island as the man.

*

The sadness on her face tore at Nicholas, knowing he was the reason for her anger and her pain.

"This came for you earlier today." Nicholas opened the top drawer and extended a cream-colored envelope toward Isabelle.

Opening the envelope, she pulled out the single sheet of paper and read it. The paper clenched tightly in her hand, she lifted her stare to Nicholas. "Surely this isn't possible. They wouldn't have replaced me already."

"That was never my intention," Nicholas said softly, unable to say anything to help salvage Isabelle's feelings. From the look she threw him, she wanted nothing of the sort from him.

"Maybe not, but what did you think would happen? Six months is a long time to be without a head cardiothoracic surgeon. I hoped it wouldn't come to this, but it was inevitable. Garner General is a busy hospital and someone has to fill the void in my absence."

He heard the frustration in her voice and wished he had something that would disperse her pain. While it was true Nicholas hadn't considered the hospital would replace Isabelle during her half-year absence, he didn't think it would become a priority. Apparently he'd thought wrong. By doing so, he jeopardized Isabelle's future career options. He made a mental note to call the Chief of Staff Kevin Aldridge to discuss the situation. Quite possibly there was something Nicholas could do to remedy the unfortunate situation. Then another idea formed in his mind that would solve the problem quite nicely.

"You could always stay here and work in the Wellfleet Isle Hospital. Our country would welcome you with open arms. The hospital would be overjoyed to have a doctor of your caliber on staff." The words were out of his mouth before Nicholas could contain himself.

Isabelle looked shocked at the offer he presented, but quickly recovered. "No, I'm afraid that would never work."

"Of course it would. You could work at the hospital and live here at the palace. It would work out well for all parties concerned."

"You mean it would work out for you quite nicely." Isabelle stopped pacing and faced him. "When did you plan on telling me? Or quite possibly you weren't going to say a word about Marissa. Though I do think she might have something to say about my living here as well."

Nicholas was confused by her response and her accusation cut him to the bone. He'd just offered her a wonderful opportunity and she seemed annoyed with the prospect.

"I won't be your mistress, let alone anyone's second choice. You are seriously delusional if you think we're going to pick back up and pretend nothing ever happened, especially now."

The silence stretched between them as realization dawned on Nicholas's face.

"Is that what you think this offer is about?"

She nodded slowly without speaking.

He rammed his hand through his hair and let out a loud exhale. "I don't recall asking you to be my mistress." The words came out sharper than intended and one quick look at her face was all he needed to see the anguish etched in her features.

"But you would have since Marissa is the one chosen to be your wife," she said softly.

For as much as he wanted to right the wrong and ease her pain, Nicholas couldn't. Isabelle was correct in assuming he wanted her as his mistress, regardless of whether he had posed the question aloud or not.

"Your highness, pardon the intrusion." Nicholas's secretary stood in the doorway. "This just arrived for you. It's marked urgent."

Nicholas motioned her into the room and took the message. "Thank you."

The woman bowed and retreated.

He looked down at the paper, reading the words contained within. "I must go. We'll finish our talk later." Nicholas turned on his heel and left the room, leaving Isabelle alone.

*

"That's where you're wrong, Nicholas. We're never going to talk about this again."

In fact, Isabelle couldn't wait to erase the memory as fast as possible. Though she'd said the words to an empty room, they were how she felt and nothing would change her mind. Nothing Nicholas could say or do would sway her from her decision.

He'd led her to believe... No, Isabelle mentally corrected herself. She'd led herself to believe they had a past, present, and future. She couldn't blame this on Nicholas, when she was the gullible one.

His place was here with the people who needed him, depended on him, and loved him. The same as she did. He needed to be here with his family. A family of which she was not a part. The tears slid down her cheeks as Isabelle buried her face in her hands.

You were my family. You were all I needed. My family needs nothing more from me than whatever boost up the social ladder my name or achievements will give them.

She moved to the window and stared out at the courtyard. As she stood there, Nicholas went out the front door and headed toward a waiting car. Nicholas climbed in, the door shut behind him, and the car went off down the driveway out of sight. A feeling of déjà vu slithered down her spine, as an icy chill settled over her skin.

I need you.

The words were so simple, yet Isabelle knew she wouldn't do it, she couldn't do it. All she had to do was pick up the phone or walk across the palace to his suite and say the words.

It would solve nothing, especially now that she knew about his intended bride-to-be and their fall engagement party. It was like a scar that wouldn't heal, raw and angry, always a painful reminder. Isabelle tried to convince herself it was his arrogance in the matter that set her nerves on edge. But the truth remained: it was his nearness that caused the rush of emotion and Isabelle knew she could never allow herself to remain on the island for any longer than necessary.

There had never been anyone else that could compare to Nicholas in her life. And if Isabelle chose to be honest with herself, there never would be. He was the only man she'd ever loved. Then lost, she reminded herself. The memories of what they shared would have to last her a lifetime. There would be no more kissing or touching or anything. But none of it mattered because no way would she reconsider becoming the mistress to the future king of Wellfleet Isle.

*

Nicholas walked out the front doors of the hospital and into the bright sunshine of the day. His head was muddled with facts and figures, none of which held his attention for more than a minute. And if his brother kept up the incessant chattering, Nicholas vowed to have him thrown to the sharks. He could barely focus at meetings, making decisions was difficult, and worse yet, Isabelle had been avoiding him quite nicely for the past week.

As he turned the corner, he came to an abrupt halt. Less than ten yards in front of him was Isabelle, seated on the bench in the courtyard.

"Ah, the fair maiden herself. I swear when the light hits her that way, she looks just like a fairy tale princess. Don't you agree big brother?" Aidan came up beside him and lightly punched him on the arm to get his attention. Little did he know, Isabelle was all Nicholas thought of lately.

"I don't believe in fairy tales. They are for children and storybooks. They have no place in the real world." But she did look wonderful. A sight for sore eyes, he thought ruefully.

"That may be, but just look at her. She looks like a princess from a fairy tale with all the children about her."

Nicholas stared across the courtyard at Isabelle. She'd volunteered to read to the children, another way of avoiding contact with Nicholas in the afternoons. She did look like a princess. With her upswept hair and brightly colored sundress, she could easily blend into any royal outing with ease. The notion took root in his brain. She was a natural as the young tots clamored for more and she willingly complied. Her laughter, once given to him freely, was now reserved for the children nestled beside her and at her feet.

She could have been someone's mother, sitting there surrounded by the littlest patients in the hospital. He imagined her holding their child on her lap, reading a story. Would it be a girl or a boy? Tow-headed or brunette?

He jammed his hands into his pockets as Isabelle laughed at something Aidan said, before his brother took her hand and kissed it loudly, causing the children to laugh with glee. Nicholas frowned, the laughter making it hard for him to focus on anything but how big a fool he'd been. The thought of her kissing another man, or sleeping with another man, was a fierce kick to the gut, sucking the air from his lungs. That Nicholas lost Isabelle years ago was his own doing. And now he'd thoroughly and cleanly repeated the process.

If he'd come back after the funeral and told her the truth would it have changed anything? Nicholas closed his eyes and drew in a deep breath. In his heart, he knew the answer. In his head, the outcome was something completely different.

With a flick of his hand, the driver brought the limousine around and Nicholas climbed into the back seat, the door closing behind him, effectively eliminating her from view.

*

Isabelle turned and caught Nicholas staring at her. She gnawed on her lip, watching the limousine pull away from the curb. Her heart leaped into her throat at the subtle reminder. How the past once more come full circle as he drove off out of view.

It was as though Nicholas couldn't wait to get away from her. He'd never love her the way she wanted him to, the way she deserved to be loved. And Isabelle wouldn't accept anything less than the whole package.

Growing up in a family that expended more energy on outward appearances than true family values taught her never to set her own desires aside for someone else. Regardless of how much she loved Nicholas, they could never be together.

It didn't matter they'd spent all those nights together. It didn't matter that Nicholas whispered sweet nothings in her ear while they made love. And it didn't matter how she felt right at this moment. What did matter was she finally realized everything she felt for Nicholas meant nothing. They had no future, despite their obvious attraction. While she couldn't ignore the fact he would always hold a small place in her heart, another part of her knew it was time to stop pretending. He would marry Marissa and together they would rule Wellfleet Isle exactly as the article stated. Isabelle had learned the hard way you couldn't miss what you truly never had.

*

The next morning Isabelle deliberately stalled as long as possible before going down to breakfast in hopes Nicholas would have eaten and gone. Unfortunately, he was still in the dining room. For the past two weeks, she'd been able to avoid sharing meals with him by dining in her suite or with Aidan, but not this morning.

"If I didn't know better, I would think you were avoiding me?" He lifted his coffee cup to his lips and took a sip, his blue eyes aimed directly at her.

"Now why would I do something like that?" She hurriedly shifted her gaze, lest he figure out how accurate his statement really was.

Isabelle never backed down from an obligation and she wasn't about to start now. When she gave her word, it meant something. She would stay and finish the job, and then be on the first plane out of Wellfleet Isle and back to Chicago.

What she didn't anticipate was feeling so comfortable in such a short time. Instead ,she'd pictured it as just another job, with a patient whose celebrity status dictated at-home private medical care. Isabelle found herself pleased to admit her reservations about taking the job in the first place were misguided. But that was where it all ended thanks to the newspaper article.

"We're two grown adults. Certainly despite our differences, we can be civil to one another at least for the remaining time I'm here." She picked up a slice of melon and put it on her plate before turning toward the array of hot foods.

"I know how upset you must be."

The ladle hit the side of the chafing dish with a loud clang as Isabelle snapped her face to his. "You know nothing about me. I'm not the same person you left behind ten years ago. A lot has changed. I've changed. So please don't insult me by pretending to think you know anything about me. Not anymore."

Isabelle tried to tamp down her anger as she finished filling her plate, and then poured a glass of juice from the sidebar. She carried the items to the door before turning back to face him.

"I think it's time you talked to your father about the surgery. He needs that surgery and the time's grown short."

"I'll have a word with him this afternoon when I return from my meeting."

"Thank you." Isabelle walked out the dining room doors and headed for the terrace. She couldn't bear the thought of being cooped up in the house, especially not with Nicholas seated across from her. But more importantly, she refused to let him see the tears that threatened. She wouldn't allow herself to shed another tear for a man who obviously wasn't worth her time or effort.

*

"I suppose Isabelle sent you in here to coerce me to have the surgery." His father folded his hands in his lap, lips pursed, ready to take on the world from the looks of things.

Nicholas sat down in the chair beside his father's bedside. "I told her I would speak with you. But it's not my decision to make. If you choose not to have the surgery, who am I to take you to task for your refusal? It was the same with mother when she didn't tell us about being ill. It was her decision in the end."

He'd never spoken with his father of his mother's passing since the day of her death.

"This is nothing like your mother's situation."

"Actually it is. Is it your intent to let this disease kill you outright when you could have the surgery and live years longer? Possibly long enough to see both your sons get married." Nicholas lifted his hand to stop his father's next question before it was asked. "That's a hypothetical question, father."

Philippe narrowed his gaze on Nicholas. "Hypothetical or not, point taken. I'll consider the surgery as I would never deign to cause you or your brother undue stress at my expense."

This was the closest thing to an apology Nicholas had ever heard from his father.

"Doctor Tandori, she's a good doctor, very caring. Pity to know she'll be leaving soon enough to go back to the States, though my having surgery would delay her departure, I would assume."

Nicholas didn't say a word. There was nothing he could say without revealing how he felt about Isabelle. And right now his father was the last person he wanted to know. He couldn't have her no matter how much he preferred otherwise. The people must come first as they had for hundreds of years. It was his duty, his responsibility, his life, even if it meant the expense of his own happiness.

His life.

The words echoed through his skull like a gunshot, reverberating off his brain. Nicholas was sick and tired of always being diplomatic, charming, never showing how bored he was, nor allowing his true feelings to rise to the surface.

Chapter Ten

"Mind if I join you?"

Isabelle looked up to find Aidan standing beside her chair. His approach so silent she would have sworn she was alone.

"Of course not, pull up a piece of beach and sit a while. I've got sandwiches, juice, and water if you're interested." She motioned to the cooler behind her the kitchen staff insisted she bring along, though she was only yards from the palace.

"Thanks, maybe later."

Aidan plopped down in the sand next to her beach chair, digging his toes into the warm sand, his gaze politely averted from her face. Isabelle knew it was out of courtesy he refrained from commenting on her puffy eyes and lackluster welcome, and for that, she was grateful.

She looked down at the romance novel on her lap, the words blurring before her eyes. Why hadn't she picked out a murder mystery or something with a gory final chapter instead of a hearts-and-flowers, he-loves-me-forever ending?

"My brother is a first-rate fool."

"You won't get an argument from me." The tears pricked at the back of her eyelids.

"For whatever its worth, he and Marissa have never even been in the same room together, let alone had a conversation." Aidan fiddled with a handful of sand, the grains sifting through his fingers.

Isabelle didn't know what to say or if she should say anything at all. She kept her gaze firmly on the horizon.

"Doctor Tandori."

Isabelle shaded her eyes with her hand and looked in the direction of the man running toward her on the deserted beach, shouting her name.

"That looks like Anton, one of the palace security guards," Aidan said, climbing quickly to his feet.

She stood, watching the man's approach as panic filled her chest.

"Doctor Tandori, you must come now. It's an emergency."

His words carried over the sand and Isabelle dropped the book and ran as quickly as she could across the beach following the security guard, Aidan following close at her heels.

They raced through the palace into the king's suite.

"Denton, what's happening?"

The male nurse was frantic, as he tried to describe what happened. Isabelle moved quickly to Philippe's side, her gaze locked on the portable bedside monitor.

"The king was out on the terrace. He came in to lie down, and then suddenly clutched at his chest, complaining of intense pain. I immediately summoned the guards to find you."

"I'm glad you did. Philippe, I need you to answer some questions for me."

Eyes still closed, King Philippe nodded, his voice faint and shaky. "You and your questions."

Isabelle lifted his hand searching for a pulse, noting the clamminess of his skin and the sweat glistening on his face.

"Tell me how you feel."

"Like an elephant is sitting on my chest. Every time I try to take a breath the pain increases. I feel nauseated, as though my lunch isn't sitting well." His words now raspy and hoarse.

His blood pressure was dropping, his pulse thready and erratic. But it was the gray pallor of his face that concerned Isabelle. "Call for an ambulance. Let them know the king is suffering from a myocardial infarction." Denton hurried off to do her bidding. She then turned back to Philippe. "We're going to the hospital and there will be no argument."

"As you wish, my dear."

"What do you need me to do?" Aidan was by her side.

"Are you sure you wouldn't prefer to wait out front for the ambulance?"

Aidan shook his head. "No, I'd rather be here with Father."

"Start an IV, and he needs more oxygen."

"Aidan?" The king lifted his hand, motioning his younger son closer.

"Yes, Father." He moved to the side of the bed, taking his father's hand in his.

"It's nice to have you home again."

"It's nice to be here, Father. Now please do as Isabelle says." Aidan leaned over the bed and gently placed a kiss on his father's brow before securing the oxygen mask. Then he quickly turned his attention toward placing an IV line in the King's left arm.

"Philippe, I want you to hold this nitroglycerin pill under your tongue. Don't chew or swallow it. Let it dissolve on its own. Are you able to do that?"

"Yes, but first I must tell you that I'll have the surgery. Whatever you need to do, I'm ready." The words were whispered.

Isabelle gave Philippe the pill, then resumed watching his vitals, the leads to the EKG in place and the test started.

Denton returned his position by the bedside. "The paramedics will be here any minute and the guards will escort them in post haste."

"Good." Isabelle kept her eyes on the screen, and then printed off the EKG strip for the paramedics.

"IV is in place, taped and secure, oxygen at high flow volume. What else do you need me to do?"

Isabelle turned toward the younger man, lowering her stethoscope. "Call your brother. We'll meet him at the hospital; tell him not to waste time getting there."

Aidan stepped from the room to place the call and returned within a few minutes with the paramedics in tow. "He's on his way."

Isabelle stepped back out of the way and watched the paramedics carefully place King Philippe on the gurney as they wheeled him from the bedroom.

"I'd like to ride with the king." Isabelle told the paramedic.

"Of course, there's room for both you and Prince Aidan."

"Thank you." Isabelle glanced down at her clothes and realized she was still wearing her shorts and a t-shirt. At present, there was no time to run to her suite and change clothes, she would have to go as she was dressed.

Looking at Philippe, her stomach plummeted. Time had officially run out for the king. This was not the way she envisioned having to proceed, but with the heart attack, they would have no choice but to go forward with the surgery. And the sooner the better.

Jumping down from the back of the ambulance, Isabelle followed the gurney through the emergency room entrance to find Nicholas pacing back and forth in front of the reception desk.

She moved forward and took hold of his arm, feeling the warmth of his skin beneath her fingers, preventing him from following the paramedics as they took Philippe into an exam room. "Let them do their job and get your father settled before you go barging in there."

He looked down at her hand on his arm, and then let out a shaky breath. "You're right, of course. What happened?"

Isabelle dropped her hand to her side and stepped back from Nicholas. She needed to focus on the man down the hall, not the one by her side.

"Your father suffered a major heart attack, though I doubt you need me to explain any of this to you."

"How serious is it?"

"Once he's stabilized, we have no choice but to proceed with surgery. I've alerted the doctors and they've started preparations. Another attack like this could kill him and that is still a distinct possibility until we've found a donor." They walked a few steps down the hallway, stopping in front of the exam room. On the other side, Philippe was being hooked up to a wide variety of machines and monitors.

Nicholas stared down at the frail man on the hospital bed through the window of the examination room.

"Once all the test results are in, I'll know where we stand."

"Do whatever necessary to save my father. No matter what." Nicholas lifted his hand to the glass panel as though willing his father to live.

*

Isabelle opened her eyes in the semi-darkness of the hospital room. She turned her head, finding Nicholas a lot closer than she thought, seated in the chair next to her. He reached out and touched her arm.

"Are you all right? You look pale."

"I'm fine. Just a bit tired, I think."

"You dozed off for a bit. I didn't want to disturb your slumber. Will he sleep the rest of the night?"

Isabelle cast a quick glance at the monitors, noting the readings on the screen. The king's levels were stable, though still above normal range. "Yes, the drugs will help to a certain degree."

"Let me take you back to the palace so you can rest. Aidan will be here with father and if anything comes up, he'll call."

"I should stay."

"No, you should go. He'll need you fresh in the morning when he awakes."

Nicholas had a point. Against her better judgment, she allowed Nicholas to escort her back to the palace, leaving Aidan at the hospital with Philippe.

Isabelle stared at the night sky outside the limousine. So many stars to make a wish upon, yet at the moment, she couldn't bring herself to think of even one. "Let me take you home" Nicholas said. If only that's what it was, instead of a temporary place to rest her head.

The limousine pulled to a stop outside the front door of the palace and Isabelle was out the door as soon as possible. "Thank you for the ride back."

"You're most welcome. But it is I who should be thanking you for your quick actions and response to my father's emergency this afternoon."

She shook her head, not wanting to accept the compliments. "I was just doing my job. Thank your brother; he was a big help in getting the IV line in place. He's very good at what he does."

"I wish to apologize to you for my lapse in judgment. It was never my intent to make you feel unwanted. My attraction to you was real, is real, but my people—"

Isabelle lifted her hand, her fingers landing gently on his mouth. She didn't want to talk about it, didn't want to think about it, and couldn't handle the thought of Nicholas blaming it on the people. "Please don't say anything. It's better off forgotten."

Nicholas reached out and placed his hand on her arm. "No, I need to tell you how sorry I am that things turned out this way. I never meant to cause you any pain."

"No one forced me into your arms or your bed, I went willingly. It took two of us to create what happened. I'm a big girl, I can handle the fallout, but I think it's best if we forget what happened while I was here. It's better that way."

"It won't be that simple," Nicholas said softly.

Isabelle lifted her hand and placed it tenderly on Nicholas's cheek, feeling the warmth of his skin beneath her fingers. "I'm afraid it has to be. What we shared in the past is over. You're a good man, Nicholas, and you'll make a great king one day. I'm sorry things weren't different. Maybe there would have been a chance, but your future is with your bri—" She shook her head, stumbling over the words. "Your future is with Marissa."

Isabelle walked off down the hallway, eager to get to her suite before her self-control shattered. She knew what she was getting into from the start, all but the part about Nicholas having a bride-to-be in the wings.

She needed to get the heck away from Wellfleet Isle as soon as possible.

*

The next morning Isabelle was up and off to the hospital before the rest of the palace began to stir. If miracles could happen, they had for Philippe. A donor heart had become available and he would soon be prepped for surgery.

Isabelle was awaiting the arrival of Nicholas and Aiden before she headed into pre-op. She didn't have to wait long before she saw Nicholas striding toward her down the hallway.

"When will the surgery commence?" he asked, all pleasantries pushed aside for the time being.

"I've got your father on the schedule for this morning. I see no reason not to move forward with the surgery. His vitals are stable and he's alert. The donor organ will arrive here within the hour."

"You will be in there every step of the way?"

"Yes, Doctor Ahmed and Doctor Madden will head up the team; I will scrub and stand by to assist as necessary and to oversee the surgery. While this is not the way I would prefer surgery to occur, we have no choice but to press forward."

Nicholas nodded. "If father would have agreed sooner, it never would have gotten to this point. But it has and we must do what is necessary. I trust you will have someone keep me apprised as to what is going on?"

"Of course I will. Now if you'll excuse me, I need to see my patient."

Nicholas trailed behind her as she headed for Philippe's hospital room.

"Good morning, Philippe. We're scheduled for eleven o'clock this morning so I'm afraid no breakfast or lunch today."

"I don't like the taste of hospital food anyway." Philippe said, as Isabelle moved closer to the bed, lifted the covers and examined his legs.

"They'll be doing tests on you this morning in preparation for the surgery. Once in the OR, you'll be given general anesthesia. After surgery…"

"Spare me the details, my dear. I would prefer not to know what you are going to do to me once I am in the OR. I'm sure it is not a pleasant surgery I am about to undergo, and as such, I have no wish to have every gruesome detail explained in depth."

"If that is what you would prefer, then I will not discuss the surgery." Isabelle would have preferred to explain every step rather than avoid any talk at all, but she would abide by Philippe's wishes in the matter. There would enough time for conversation afterwards.

"When can I go home?"

"You will be taken to the ICU after surgery for about one to three days. After that, you'll be moved to the Step Down ICU for another five to seven days. Then if all goes well, you can go home at that point. But you're still looking at about three months before you'll start feeling like yourself again as well."

"The old normal or the new normal?"

"The new normal. You owe me that dance you promised, remember?"

Philippe's eyes lit up and he smiled wanly. "That I do. Okay, when can we get this process moving?"

"The next time I see you will be in the operating room," Isabelle told him.

*

Isabelle scrubbed up at the stainless steel sink and mentally ran through the surgery in her head. Pulling on the blue gown, she tied the bottom half of the mask across the back of her neck and headed into the operating room.

"Any last minute questions?" Isabelle looked down at Philippe on the operating table; a bevy of wires and tubes connected him to the machines necessary for the surgery.

"I'm holding you accountable for getting me through this."

"You have my word, your highness. I'll be right here for the whole thing." She smiled at him, though her heart was pounding in her chest. He had to come through the surgery; otherwise Isabelle didn't know what she'd do if she had to tell Nicholas any bad news.

Isabelle nodded to the anesthesiologist. "Close your eyes and rest now. I'll see you later."

She sent up a short prayer to the powers that be to keep the king safe and strong.

*

Nicholas paced back and forth across the waiting room until he felt as though he would go insane if someone didn't come tell him something. He couldn't sit, couldn't focus on the television set broadcasting some inane talk show in the corner of the room, and couldn't wait for someone to update them. A nurse had come out at various times letting them know everything was going as expected, his father was doing well and Doctor Tandori would be out as soon as the surgery was over to talk to them.

This was what he had trained for, to be in the operating room, not standing by idly waiting for someone to update him. All those years of classes, then residency, and not an ounce of it put to good use. Nicholas looked down at his hands, at the trembling fingers that performed more surgeries then he cared to count. But it had been a decade since he's donned the surgical scrubs, washed up at the sink, and held a scalpel in his hand. He'd done it all to save people and look where it had gotten him. As far removed as possible from the operating room.

He'd just completed another lap of the private waiting room when Isabelle came through the doors, pulling her surgical cap from her head. Nicholas cut his steps short and hurried toward her, Aidan and Denton following in his wake.

*

"Tell me Father is all right?" Nicholas asked.

Isabelle nodded. "Philippe is stable and in recovery. The surgery went well, but as you know, the next twenty-four hours will be critical."

"When can I see him?" Nicholas asked impatiently.

Isabelle turned and looked at the clock on the waiting room wall. "Minimum I would say is in another three hours. He's still in Recovery at present. Why don't you go get something to eat and then come back later in the evening. You look as though you could use a break."

"Excuse me, Doctor Tandori, if the surgery is a success, how soon can he come home?" Denton asked.

"Once we know he is out of the woods, I would estimate a good ten days." Isabelle knew how close the man was with the king, spending the better part of his life as the king's aide and later personal nurse.

Aidan and Denton moved back toward the chairs in the waiting room, clearly relieved at the news.

"I appreciate that whatever your feelings are toward me, you didn't allow them to cloud your judgment in your decision to perform surgery on my father."

It was all Isabelle could do not to haul off and smack Nicholas for his callous remark. The stupid arrogant jerk. How dare he even begin to think she would compromise her standards because of him? She mentally counted to ten before answering.

"Don't flatter yourself, Nicholas. I did what I had to do to save your father. You never entered my mind at any point before, during or after the surgery. Now if you'll excuse me, I have to get back to my patient."

Isabelle started to walk back to the surgical lounge, but Nicholas gently grabbed her arm, pulling her to a halt. "Thank you. I owe you my life."

She looked down at his hand on her arm and then shook her head. "No, your highness, you don't owe me a thing. Not anymore." Disengaging her arm from his, Isabelle walked away without looking back as the automatic doors to the surgical suite shut behind her.

*

The king leaned back against the pillows. "Will I live?"

Looping the stethoscope around her neck, Isabelle made a quick note on the medical chart and tried to hide her smile. "For quite a few more years as long as you follow doctor's orders."

"I suppose you'll be heading back to the States now that my surgery is complete and I'm about to head home? Though I hope you won't leave until I am once again ensconced in the palace."

The words she wanted to say but couldn't were stuck in her throat so Isabelle simply nodded.

"Are you going to tell Nicholas about the baby before you leave?"

Her head came up so fast the room spun before her, and Isabelle grabbed the edge of the chair for support. "I don't know what you're talking about."

"I think you do, my dear. Ten years ago, the night Nicholas left you and returned home to Wellfleet. You miscarried the child even though you were able to call for the paramedics."

Isabelle sank down in the chair beside the bed for fear her legs would collapse from under her. How was it possible he knew? She turned her face from his, trying to hide the truth.

"How do you know about that? No one knows."

The king took her hand in his. "There are a great many perks to being a royal. People will jump through hoops to do your bidding. Did you think we didn't know about you and Nicholas living together?"

"We?" She whispered.

"Queen Julia and I. We had no secrets between us, save for one."

"But I didn't know about any of you," she replied honestly. "I didn't know until Nicholas came to Chicago to offer me the position here."

King Philippe nodded. "Yes, that is true."

"Are you going to tell him?" Isabelle changed tactics with the conversation, then gently placed her fingers on the king's wrist, ready to take his pulse. She paused, waiting for his answer.

Philippe shrugged and seemed to contemplate her question before responding. "We all have our secrets to bear, don't you agree?"

Isabelle looked at him oddly. Maybe it was the way he was looking at her, as if seeing something she didn't want him to.

"Sometimes, my dear, a secret is kept because the bearer feels it is the right thing to do under the circumstances. But the real question is, is it the right thing for whom? The one he's trying to protect, or in reality, is he trying to protect his own self. Either one will most certainly change the final outcome."

*

Nicholas leaned back against the wall in the corridor; out of sight should Isabelle come out of his father's room and see him standing there. She miscarried their baby the same day he'd been called back to Wellfleet Isle when his mother passed away. The blood roared in his ears as he fought to stay upright. How dare she not tell him the news of her pregnancy. Nicholas had a right to know he would have been a father. A father to a baby that never had the opportunity to be born.

He wished he could see her face while she answered his father's questions. To see if she were truthful. But deep in his heart Nicholas knew she wouldn't lie about something so important. It wasn't in her nature.

Quite possibly it was his fault that Isabelle miscarried? Possibly because of the way he left her standing there alone? Possibly because she had no one to turn to in times of need. And, as such, her miscarriage was the end result. The anger faded into the background as guilt ate at him, gnawing on his insides. He abandoned her when she needed him most. Nicholas didn't want to think about Isabelle alone and vulnerable in their apartment, couldn't envision the thoughts that went through her head as she waited for the paramedics. The fear she might lose their child and the realization when she did. Was it any wonder she hated him so much?

Nicholas waited until he was sure Isabelle had left the hospital and gone back to the palace before entering his father's hospital room.

"Good news, my son. I am to be discharged tomorrow."

"That's wonderful, father. It'll be good to have you home again." His thoughts distracted, he missed what the king was saying until the words "assume the throne" caught Nicholas's ear.

"I beg your pardon; would you repeat that last part?"

Philippe chuckled. "I said I'll be stepping down at the end of this year and you will assume the crown. It's been time for quite a while, but I hoped things would be different. Now that Aidan is here, everything will fall into place quite nicely. But I see something is bothering you."

"It's nothing, father. I'm sure it'll all work itself out in the end."

"And if it doesn't?"

"Then it wasn't meant to be. As you say, duty must come first before family."

King Philippe shook his head. "You know I believed that by allowing you to go to the States for your schooling it would somehow let you sow your wild oats, get the outrageous notion out of your head that you wanted to be a doctor, and you would come home happy with how your life was ordained for you."

"You think that was why I went to Georgetown, to sow my wild oats. Like it was a precursor to coming back here, getting married, and running the country? Father, you are sadly mistaken."

The king lifted his hand. "Please Nicholas, allow me to finish. I admit I was a fool in that respect. I see now you went there to further a career that meant the world to you. A career that was taken from you when circumstances changed here on the island. Maybe if I would have paid more attention to my family, listened to what they really wanted and needed, I wouldn't have lost your mother."

"What happened to her was not your fault." Nicholas had never heard his father talk like this before.

"No, but maybe if I'd been more attentive to her needs, I would have seen there was a problem well in advance."

"I don't understand what that has to do with me," Nicholas said.

"I'm talking about Doctor Tandori."

Isabelle.

Nicholas's stomach clenched at the way they parted. She'd barely said a dozen words to him since that day. It was as though she was avoiding his visits to the hospitals and made sure to be scarce whenever he was around. And at the palace she was no different.

"What are you going to do about her?"

"There isn't anything to do about her. She'll be leaving for the States within the next week."

"May I offer a suggestion?" Philippe's steely eyed stare was now firmly fixated on Nicholas.

"Of course, Father." Right now, he'd listen to anything that might bring about a resolution to the situation. Though he doubted Isabelle felt the same way. Her intentions were clear in regard to how she felt about him.

"I suggest you run out that door, find the woman, and beg her forgiveness before it's too late."

Nicholas shook his head in confusion. "I don't understand. Just a minute ago, you told me I had to step up to the plate and assume the role of king full-time because you were stepping down. Now you are telling me to go after Isabelle. What good is that if I can't be with her? And she's already made it clear she won't be with me any other way. She won't be my mistress."

The king raised an eyebrow at Nicholas's last statement. "You need to do whatever your heart is telling you to do. But I'm telling you not to let the best thing you've ever had slip away. Remember son, you are the future king and as such, you make the rules."

*

If this were well and truly his life, then why couldn't Nicholas live it as he saw fit?

Having her on Wellfleet Isle to care for his father had been his primary motive in the beginning. Later on it somehow morphed into a totally different reason altogether. He wanted her here because of himself. Nicholas wanted someone to spar with him when it came to decision making, not smile, nod, and agree. And with Isabelle, Nicholas was sure she wouldn't concede any point without a fair fight. If truth be told, it was Isabelle he wanted by his side, to raise his children here, with her as their mother, take them to the same beach his mother had taken him and Aidan for picnics on the sand. Nicholas couldn't think of anything else he wanted more in life.

He wanted her here because he loved her. He loved Isabelle from her bright pink painted toenails to the top of her curly auburn head.

Love.

He loved Isabelle as he had from the moment their eyes met and had never stopped loving her. Nothing changed in all that time, nothing except...everything.

What if...

Nicholas came to a screeching halt in the corridor outside his father's hospital room, an idea firmly taking shape in his brain. As long as he did what was expected of his position, Nicholas would not disappoint his father. Nor would he disappoint the people of his country. And right now, both weighed heavily on his mind. Slamming his hand down on the railing, Nicholas bit back the string of curse words that rose combined with the pain in his palm.

Chapter Eleven

Isabel couldn't believe the time had drawn to a close. It seemed only yesterday when she'd gotten her first glimpse of the palace. As hard as she tried to tell herself otherwise, she'd come to love the small island country and its inhabitants. Almost as much as the realization that she loved Nicholas.

Her knees threatened to buckle as her breath caught in her throat. Isabelle closed her eyes and fought the tears. Shaking her head, she wouldn't allow herself to cry over what might have been and what never would be again.

Isabelle never felt this way about any other man and deep down inside knew she never would again. Nicholas Corsairs was one of a kind. He was the first man she'd ever slept with and, in her wishful girlish dreams, hoped he would be the last. No use wishing for something that wouldn't happen. She pinned her hopes on the impossible. Isabelle had come full circle, something else she vowed would never happen. She was still in love with Nicholas.

"Are you sure I can't convince you to stay?" Aidan walked her to the limousine, his normally smiling face serious for a change.

Isabelle shook her head. "No, I have to leave. Your father is recovering beautifully, which means my job is finished."

"Nicholas is a fool to let you go."

"Please take care of yourself. I know you're going to be a wonderful addition to the hospital and more importantly to the people of Wellfleet Isle." She hugged Aidan tightly, pressed a kiss to his cheek, and then stepped back. "If you're ever in Chicago, give me a call."

The younger man smiled. 'You can count on it. I'll take you to some of my favorite haunts. We'll set the paparazzi on its ear."

Settling herself back on the plush leather seat of the limousine, Isabelle looked out the window at the view as the palace faded into the background. The lush greenery graced the roadside, the huge white hibiscus in full bloom dotted the landscape, and the bright blue waters of the Caribbean could be seen peeking out from between the branches. Everything the same as it was upon her arrival. Everything except Isabelle.

This time she was the one walking away and leaving, not Nicholas. Isabelle closed her eyes and drew in a ragged breath. It wasn't supposed to be like this. She wasn't supposed to fall in love with him again. As she stepped out of the air-conditioned limousine and onto the private runway, the ocean breeze caressed her face.

She didn't know how she was going to walk away and heal the gigantic hole in her heart. Maybe it was better to hurt like the devil rather than feel nothing at all. At least this way, Isabelle knew she could feel pain, bittersweet as it was.

Crossing the tarmac, she fought the urge to turn around and look behind her to see if Nicholas was coming to stop her departure. But she didn't dare turn around for fear of what she wouldn't see. As she climbed the steps to the plane, Isabelle found herself wishing things could be different. But she was a commoner and he was… Nicholas was the future king of Wellfleet Isle. And nothing would ever change that fact.

Yet Isabelle found her gaze drawn to the closed door of the jet time and again as the plane sat on the runway waiting for clearance. With a rueful shake of her head, she pulled her thoughts to the moment at hand—wool gathering, as Philippe liked to say. Something Isabelle found herself doing a lot more of in past weeks.

She settled herself in the seat and fastened the seatbelt across her lap. For the first time in a long time, the thought of take-off didn't scare her. In fact, she welcomed it. The sooner the plane left the ground the better. Granted, that also meant the farther away from Wellfleet Isle the better.

The view outside the airplane window blurred as the plane picked up speed and her eyes filled with tears. Isabelle pulled a tissue from her pocket and began to dab at her eyes as the tears slid down her cheeks unchecked. The sound of the engines grew louder as the plane taxied down the runway, away from the main terminal.

Swiping at the tears, Isabelle was furious with herself for allowing the Corsairs to become so ingrained in her daily life. She'd never allowed herself to become emotionally invested with a patient, and Philippe should have been no different. Whatever happened on the island had changed Isabelle. She was a different person, with different needs and only time would tell how she'd move forward in order to encompass them.

Isabelle peered out the window and noticed they were turning in a circle, headed back up the runway. As she watched, the main terminal building came back into view.

She fumbled to unfasten her seatbelt and rose from the chair, headed toward the front of the plane at the same time the flight attendant came out from the galley.

"Is there a reason why we're back at the gate?"

The flight attendant didn't say a word, just smiled and pulled aside the curtain as Nicholas walked through the galley into the main section of the plane.

"Yes. I'm the reason your flight has been interrupted."

"I don't understand." Isabelle shook her head and took a step back, bumping her hip on the edge of the seat in her haste to put some space between her and Nicholas. What was he doing here? According to his calendar, he should've been attending a meeting on the other side of the island. Not standing right smack dab in front of her. And definitely not looking as good as he did right at this very moment. The scent of his aftershave tickled her nose as he moved closer.

"I couldn't let you leave."

"I beg your pardon?" Isabelle wasn't certain she'd heard him correctly. "My job here is finished. Your father is healing quite nicely from his surgery so there is no need for me to stay any longer."

"I need you."

All right, now Isabelle knew she must be going crazy since there was no way Nicholas could have just said he needed her. It wasn't possible.

She shook her head. "No, you don't."

"Yes, I do." He moved forward and took her hand in his, meshing their fingers together. "I need you to stay, Isabelle. For my sake, no one else."

"But you're going to marry Marissa. She'll be the next queen of Wellfleet Isle." Isabelle tried to concentrate, but all she could feel was the warmth of his hand on hers.

It was Nicholas's turn to shake his head. "How am I to marry someone I don't love? For what is a marriage if it only exists for the paper it is printed on. I spoke with Marissa last night, calling off the engagement, letting her know I was not able to marry her when my heart belonged to another. I love you, Isabelle Tandori. Only you."

"You're just saying that, you don't mean it." She plopped down hard on the edge of the seat, unable to fathom what Nicholas was telling her.

"I'm sorry I left you ten years ago. It was never my intention to just walk away, but once I returned to Wellfleet, everything was different. It wasn't until you came back here with me that I realized the hole in my heart wasn't caused by my mother's death and my father's illness. It was because you weren't here standing beside me every step of the way."

Isabelle's eyes filled with tears and she dashed at them with the back of her hand.

"Isabelle, I know about the miscarriage. I overheard you and my father talking in the hospital. And I know you'll never forgive me for not being by your side when it happened and not helping you through the long, dark hours that followed. But I am here now and I will be for the rest of your life if you'll have me."

"But your family, your people."

"They mean nothing to me without you by my side. And as such I am willing to give up the throne to Aidan if that is the only way you'll marry me." Nicholas dropped to one knee before her and took her hand in his.

"Doctor Isabelle Tandori, I love you and ask that you do me the honor of becoming my wife. I came straight here and didn't have time to pick out a ring for you. But will you marry me anyway?"

The sound of someone clearing his throat caused Isabelle to lift her gaze and look down the aisle, stunned at who she saw standing there.

"Philippe! You shouldn't be out of bed like this. You've just come through major surgery."

"My doctor tells me I'm healing quite nicely." Philippe held out a small blue velvet box to Nicholas. "Try this, my son. Women tend to be more receptive when you have the jewelry in hand."

Nicholas took the box and lifted the lid revealing the antique ring inside. "Father, but how did you know?"

"I may be old and infirm, but I'm not blind. The love you feel for Isabelle is as strong as the love you feel for your country. Your mother would be overjoyed at the idea. She would have passed this down to you for your own bride if she'd lived."

Nicholas lifted the ring from its resting place on the velvet. The antique gold filigree band with the marquis cut diamond sparkled brightly in the afternoon sun.

He looked back at his father, and then turned to Isabelle.

"I believe you still owe me an answer."

She wanted to believe him, she really did. But right now her thoughts were in a whirlwind. He loved her, but he loved his people. How would they ever make this work?

"Tell me you don't love me, Isabelle. If that is the case, you may leave Wellfleet Isle and I'll never bother you again."

Nicholas waited for her denial, but Isabelle couldn't say the words. As much as she wanted to refute his claim, she couldn't. She knew without a doubt that she loved him. She always had and always would.

"Yes, I love you, and yes of course I'll marry you."

Epilogue

"Tell me again."

"I love you. I love you. I love you." Isabelle leaned forward and pressed a tender kiss to Nicholas's mouth.

He sighed. "I'll never grow tired of hearing the words pass your lips."

Isabelle tipped her head back, exposing her slender neck to his view and watched the glittering lights swirl past. Nicholas pressed his lips to her throat, eliciting a soft groan from his new bride. The sound was doing crazy things to his lower anatomy.

"What are you looking at up there?" He murmured, trailing kisses up to her earlobe.

"I'm looking at the way the lights sparkle. The whole room looks like a fairy tale setting. I can't believe you did this all by yourself."

"I wouldn't say that. I did have some help in pulling the wedding together on such short notice." A lot of help if the truth be known, Nicholas mused. Otherwise, he might have found himself having to learn the difference between white, antique white, ecru, and a host of other colors he hadn't known existed. White was white in his opinion. Besides, he still would have been just as happy eloping to Vegas, but unfortunately that wasn't an option.

With her upswept hair, the small spray of island flowers nestled among the curls and the flowing white wedding gown, Isabelle looked like a fairy princess herself. He could barely take his eyes off her for fear she would disappear from sight, never to be seen again.

"It wouldn't have been so short if you'd have agreed to a longer engagement." Isabelle chided.

Nicholas shook his head. "No I'm tired of sleeping alone. I want my beautiful new wife in bed next to me, waking up with me every morning so I can kiss her lips and make sweet love to her whenever I want. As it is, you were the one who put the stipulation out there that we were not going to have sex again until we were married. Though I do seem to recall a most enjoyable midnight tryst on the beach a few nights ago. And I still have sand in places I don't think there should be."

Isabelle pursed her lips. "*Shhh.* That's supposed to be our little secret. And you expect me to believe that no sex for almost one week could bring you to your knees, the future king of Wellfleet Isle?"

Nicholas lowered his head and ran his tongue over the edge of her ear, feeling her shiver in response. "What I expect is that my wife, the future queen, will find an inventive way to make it up to me for causing me to wait those seven long days."

"I'm sure something will come to mind." Leaning forward, Isabelle pressed her mouth to his, and Nicholas tamped down the instant rush of arousal that coursed through his body. The mere touch of her sent his hormones into overdrive and today was no different. Nicholas wanted his wife, wanted to slowly strip the lace wedding gown from her body, kiss every inch of her exposed flesh, and bury himself within her. But he knew he would have to wait till the events of the day were over.

"Though it might be more fun to wait until we are on our honeymoon."

"I strongly doubt I will be able to wait that long. Though I did pack a gift for you in the luggage. A small scrap of lace I believe you found enchanting in one of the shop windows in town."

"That is so sweet of you. I'll enjoy wearing it for you on our honeymoon."

"And I'll enjoy removing it from your body." He leaned forward and gave her a deep kiss. When Nicholas lifted his head, he was pleased to find Isabelle as affected as he was. He hoped that would never change between them.

In three days, they would leave for an extended two-week honeymoon in Hawaii, and Nicholas was looking forward to every uninterrupted moment alone with Isabelle, something they'd been unable to find at the palace as of late. Aidan would fill in for Nicholas in his absence and see to his father's recovery at the same time. Life had come full circle with his family now all under one roof.

"Excuse the intrusion, my son, but I do believe your wife owes me a dance."

King Philippe stood next to them on the dance floor, resplendent in a black tuxedo, his once pale face now tanned and healthy, all due in part to Isabelle and the heart transplant surgery.

Nicholas looked from his father to Isabelle. He couldn't remember the last time the king took a turn on the dance floor or willingly participated in any activity since his mother's passing. Then again, it had been quite a while since his father was willing to make any public appearances due to his declining health. Begrudgingly releasing his wife, Nicholas took a step back, bowed to the king, then hugged him tightly. Turning to Isabelle, he said, "I shall see you later, my love."

She curtsied. "I look forward to it, your highness."

With a rueful shake of his head, Nicholas walked off the dance floor.

"So my dear, I think it's high time you started calling me Father." The king executed a quick turn and Isabelle's gown floated out behind her on the dance floor.

"Actually, I was thinking more along the line of grandfather or perhaps gramps might be better."

King Philippe missed a step and came to an abrupt halt on the marble dance floor; his surprised gaze caught on Isabelle's smiling face.

"Gramps?" The words came out more like a strained croak. His mouth gaped open, then the king quickly recovered his composure. "Oh, I think not. That is most undignified. Wait, are you saying that you—"

"Yes, I hope that won't be a problem?" Isabelle looked over the king's shoulder at her husband standing on the sidelines with Prince Aidan and smiled.

"Oh, my darling daughter-in-law, that is the most wonderful news ever." The king pulled her close, kissing her on the cheek before enveloping Isabelle in a tight hug, and then released her with a quick look around the room. Isabelle politely ignored the sheen of tears glistening in his eyes.

*

Isabelle stepped back into the circle of the king's arms and Nicholas watched them waltz gracefully around the ballroom dance floor. Accepting the flute of champagne from the passing server, he took a sip all the while staring at his bride. She was radiant, the most beautiful woman Nicholas had ever seen and now she was his wife. And soon to be the mother of his firstborn child. Tonight Nicholas planned to show her just how much he loved her and make up for all the lost time they'd missed being apart.

Conversation ceased as the guests around him stopped what they were doing. Those who were still dancing took a step back in order to give the king and his dance partner the floor. But everyone was staring in awe at the sight of the newly recovered King of Wellfleet Isle as he stepped in time to the music with his new daughter-in-law, Princess Isabelle Corsairs, or more commonly known as Doctor Isabelle Tandori Corsairs, head of the new cardiovascular care unit at Wellfleet Isle Hospital.

Author Bio

Patti Shenberger loves creating a happily ever after story as much as she loves reading one. She's been married for over thirty years to her wonderful hubby Randy, is a proud mom to Amanda and Brian, and a proud mother-in-law to James and Bobbi. When not writing, Patti can be found curled up with a good book, whiling away the hours and getting lost in the romance. For more info, please visit www.pattishenberger.com.

In the mood for more Crimson Romance? Check out *Act of Love* by Pan Zador at *CrimsonRomance.com*.